DOOMSDAY EVE

DOOMSDAY EVE

ROBERT MOORE WILLIAMS

WILDSIDE PRESS

Published by Wildside Press LLC.
www.wildsidebooks.com

CHAPTER I

The legends clustering around the new people began before the war, while the man who started the group, old Jal Jonnor, was alive, but they received their greatest circulation during the conflict.

If the war is long and the fighting is bitter, with neither side able to achieve victory or even a substantial advantage, soldiers eventually begin to tell strange stories of sights seen when death is near, of miraculous deliveries from destruction, of impossible ships seen above the Earth, and even of non-human allies fighting on their side. Psychologists, given to believing only what they can see, feel, hear, or measure, generally have credited these stories to hallucinations resulting from long-sustained stress, or, in the case of the non-human allies, to plain, wishful thinking rising out of a deep feeling of insecurity. What psychologist was ever willing to believe that an angel suddenly took over the controls of a falling fighting plane, righting the ship and bringing it down to Earth in a crash landing that enabled the wounded pilot to crawl away, then curing the wound the pilot had sustained?

Red-Dog Jimmie Thurman swore this happened to him. He had tangled with an Asian fighter group escorting a hot, high level bomber over the north pole. This was in the early days of the war when such bombers still slipped through the defenses occasionally. Red-Dog Jimmie Thurman had got one of the fighters with a single burst from his guns and was pushing his jet straight up at the soft belly of the bomber far overhead when a shell, from an Asian fighter that he had not seen, knocked off half of his right wing. A fragment of the exploding shell hit him in the right shoulder, mangling the flesh and the bone.

Spinning like a leaf being whirled over and over in a hurricane, the plane started the long plunge downward toward the polar ice cap below. Jimmie couldn't work the seat ejection mechanism because of his broken arm.

Just before the ship crashed, he realized that someone else was in the cockpit with him, fighting to take over the controls. Since Jimmie was still in the seat, this was not easy, but somehow the other one had managed, not only to take over the controls, but had been able to bring the ship down in a crash landing. The other one pulled Jimmie out of the burning wreck. Then, discovering Jimmie's broken, mangled shoulder, "it" had cured it.

At least this was the story Red-Dog Jimmie Thurman had told after a helicopter had picked him up and had taken him back to his base. He was very stubborn about it, defiantly insisting that someone else had brought the plane down. The only conclusion Jimmie had been able to reach about the other one in the cockpit with him—he did not know whether it was male or female—was that it had been one of the new people.

When the psychos had asked him how another human being could have gotten into a falling plane while it was still thousands of feet in the air, Jimmie had had no answer, except to point out that since the new people were apparently able to accomplish feats beyond the power of an ordinary mortal, they were probably not human.

This comment had marked him as permanently unfit for flight duty. Jimmie began to grieve his heart out at this, for he had really loved flying. Then he began to wonder why the new people—presuming they existed—would save his life at the cost of his sanity. He went over the hill a year later.

With Spike Larson it was different. Larson was the commander of an atomic-powered submarine operating in the Persian Gulf. He was lying doggo on the bottom waiting for a fat convoy that should be hugging the shore when three destroyers smelled him out. Larson never knew quite how they had spotted him, but he was in shallow water and, when the first depth charges went off, he knew he had to head for the depths.

With charges on the port side making his plates creak, he headed for the channel. The scanning beam reported rocks dead ahead. Swiftly checking his charts, he discovered that no such rocks existed.

Cursing, Larson flung the charts across the room. Either they were wrong or the bottom here had shifted. A boom ahead told him it made no difference. His escape had been cut off by a destroyer in the channel.

"We'll take her up and fight it out on the surface," he told the lieutenant with him.

The officer's face went white at the order. But he was a navy man. "Aye, sir," he said.

"I would recommend otherwise, commander," another voice spoke.

Larson and the lieutenant froze. There was no one else in the control room. When Larson finally managed to turn his head, he found he was wrong in his belief that no one else was in the control room.

Telling the story later, to a naval board of inquiry, he said. "She was standing right there beside me, all in shining white, the most beautiful woman I have ever seen. I was too dazed to act, too bewildered to think. A woman on my ship! And what a woman! While I stood there like a dummy, she stepped forward to the controls. 'With your permission, commander, there is a new channel close inshore that does not show on the charts. The bottom here has shifted quite a lot since this area was last mapped. The destroyers will not dare follow us into the new channel, even if they know of its existence, because of the danger from rocks on one side and from sand banks on the other. If you will give me permission to con the ship—'"

"All I could do was nod," Larson reported to the board of inquiry. "As it turned out, this was the last command I ever gave in all my life. She turned the nose of the sub seventy degrees, pulled in the scope, shut off the depth finders and the sonar, and sent us up until we were almost breaking the surface. While she was doing all this, she also dodged two depth charges that should have got us. She scraped paint off our port bow on a set of rocks that should have snatched the guts out of us; she dodged a sandy bottom on our starboard where we ought to have hung up like sitting ducks under the guns of the destroyers, but she took us out of that hole and into deep water. Then she turned the controls back to Lieutenant Thompson, and said, 'Thank you, commander. I'm sure you can handle the situation very competently from now on.'"

The members of the board of inquiry were leaning forward in their chairs so as not to miss a word of Larson's report. When he had finished, the senior member, an admiral, asked breathlessly, "And then what happened to her, commander?"

"She vanished," Larson said.

The admiral collapsed like a punctured balloon.

"Lieutenant Thompson will back up every word I have said," Larson continued. He shook his head to indicate that he still couldn't understand it, though he had thought of little else since the day it had happened.

"Who do you think she was, commander?" a member of the board asked.

"I think she was one of the new people," Larson answered. His voice was firm but he was still shaking his head when he walked out of the room where the board had met.

They gave him shore duty. The psychos did all they could for him, but something seemed to have snapped inside his brain. Eight months later he deserted.

* * * *

Then there was the story of Colonel Edward Grant, USAF. Grant was the only man aboard the new Earth satellite station. He was the only man aboard because at that time no way had been found to build and to launch a satellite that would carry more than one passenger. In fact, no way had been found to do more than launch such a station and get it into its orbit. It could not return because it could not carry enough fuel for the return journey. A spaceship was being built which would carry additional fuel and food supplies to it, but this vessel was not yet completed when the satellite was launched.

Grant, who had flown everything with wings, volunteered to ride with the station and put it in its orbit, knowing that when the power was exhausted he might be marooned in space forever.

However, neither he nor anyone else had anticipated that he would be marooned. This eventuality had only occurred when the production demands of the new war forced a halt on the construction of his rescue ship.

Colonel Grant became the loneliest man in the history of Earth. The stars were his companions. Only the moon kept him company. He would remain a lonely Flying Dutchman of the sky, until the end of the war permitted finishing the ship that would bring him relief. Or forever—whichever came first.

It was inevitable that the Asians would get the idea that he was spying on them as he passed in his regular orbit far above their heads. In reality, this was sheer nonsense; he was much too high to make out any military details of any importance whatsoever. Also, they were taking full advantage of his broadcasts of scientific information, which could be obtained by tuning in to the bands he used.

In an effort to remove this imagined menace from the sky above them, the Asians fired a rocket torpedo at his satellite.

Colonel Grant, reporting later on what had happened, said, "That torpedo must have been on its way, when the little man appeared on my satellite. He told me about the rocket that was coming my way. I told him this was very interesting but that I didn't see what the hell I could do about it. The station had no power and couldn't be moved. I didn't even have a chute, and even if I had had one I couldn't have used it. Anybody who jumped from that height would have frozen to death long before he reached enough air to sustain life. Describe the little man for you? Sure, general. He looked like a miniature Moses, white beard, glittering eyes and everything else. No, general, I never saw Moses. Clothes? A loin cloth, general. No, sir I am not making light of the dignity of this court, I am telling in the words at my command what I saw happen with my own eyes."

At this point, the colonel's voice became a little stiff. The general shut up. A man who had done what Grant had done might snap a general's head off and get away with it.

"What happened next? The miniature Moses told me he was going to land the satellite. He said that even if they missed with this torpedo they would be sure to try again, for no reason except to give the morale of their own people a big boost."

"Land the satellite, colonel?" the general asked again. "But as I understand it, the station was without power!"

"You understand the situation correctly, general. But that was what he said and that was what he did. In as neat a landing as I ever saw. And if you don't believe me, you can go look for yourself."

The space satellite sitting in the middle of a Kansas wheat field was evidence that could not be ignored. It was solid, it was metal, it was real. Colonel Grant might have gone wacky from the stress of remaining too long in space, but the station, at least, had remained sane. Power must have been used to move it. But what power?

Colonel Grant could not answer the question of what happened to the miniature Moses after the station had been landed. He flung up his hands. "Moses went the same way he came, without me seeing him."

On the basis of Grant's report, an investigation was begun. A vast mass of data was assembled, some of it dating from the time of Jal Jonnor, but when no practical results were immediately forthcoming, the project was shelved, at least temporarily. Its manpower was desperately needed for other purposes. Men fighting for their lives have no time to think of the future.

This dusty, forgotten mass of data was exhumed by a tall, lean man named Kurt Zen, a colonel of intelligence, who had a reputation for daring even among that elite band of men who daily looked death in the face.

Zen was assigned to this investigation, not only because of his reputation, but because the stories of the new people had increased in number to the point where they had to be given some credence. Also, they became more fantastic in content. For instance, a bomber pilot insisted that a woman had ridden on the wing of his ship all the way to Asia, dropping from the plane in the highlands of western China. Zen regarded this story as obvious hallucination. Much of the data about the new people belonged in this category. He morosely wondered if it was possible to tell where reality left off and hallucination began. The colonel soon discovered that his job was not going to be as easy as he'd hoped.

Aside from the stories told by the soldiers—and the Asian fighting men also had their tales to tell—only one thing was certain: if the new people existed at all, they were very elusive. Only the grave of the man who had founded the group, old Jal Jonnor, was still to be found in the high Sierras of California. Zen did not go looking for this grave, but he saw photographs of it. He also studied the biographies that had been compiled on this colossal but enigmatical figure. Were the grave and the thick files the only remaining evidence that at least one human had dared to dream of a new day? Zen did not think so. Most of all, he longed to capture one of the new people for questioning.

Then, in a daring coup that was intended to strike a spearhead at the heart of America, Cuso, the top Asian fighting leader, and thousands of tough Asian paratroopers floated down into the mountains between British Columbia and the United States.

Cuso and his men, hiding out in the high mountain ranges, resisted all efforts to dislodge them. They became a festering thorn in the side of America, a threat that was not quite big enough to take seriously, or slight enough to overlook. He was hidden so deep in the mountain caverns that he could not be bombed out and the terrain was so rugged that his paratroopers could withstand the assault of a full army.

As his men began making forays into the lower ranges, searching for food and women, the inhabitants of the area fled in terror.

This was the situation when Kurt Zen accompanied a body of troops up the last fairly good trail toward Cuso's hidden lair. Neither the troops nor Cuso really interested him. What interested him was an army nurse with the medical detachment. He suspected this nurse was one of the new people.

In months of patient, painstaking work, she was the only good lead to this group that he had uncovered.

He was going up a steep mountain trail, with troops ahead and behind, when something that sounded like a wounded lion began to cough in the sky overhead.

CHAPTER II

Kurt Zen heard the lion cough in the sky overhead. He knew that it would hit in about four minutes and that it would seem to open a tunnel upward from hell, that the mountains would shake and tremble, that the air would vibrate and rattle as if a dozen thunderbolts had exploded at the same instant, and that a good number of the troops laboriously circling the incline of the ridge above would die.

He knew that more of them would die a horrible lingering death as a result of the radioactivity that would be released by the blast.

"Pardon me, Nedra," he said to the nurse, who was just ahead of him.

She had stopped to stare upward.

"Hit the dirt!" Zen yelled at the troops. A few had already heard the lion cough in the sky and had begun to take cover, following the pattern of experienced fighters who never need an order to dive for the nearest hole. He saw, as he shouted, that the number who had already begun to hit the dirt was pitifully few and he knew the reason for this. Most of these men were green conscripts on their first fighting mission, the results of digging deep into a population that had already been scoured to the bone for manpower—and for everything else. Conscripts were likely to stare at the sky and die with their mouths open.

"What is it?" the girl asked. "What's wrong?"

"Don't you hear that blooper in the sky overhead?"

"No. That is, I heard something make a noise up there. But—" Mixed emotions moved across her face but fear was not among them. Instead, she seemed to be curious. "But what is a blooper?"

From a nurse, or from any living American, such a question was incredible. Zen stared at her in amazement.

"Did I say the wrong thing, ask the wrong question?"

"You sure did," Zen answered. "Come on."

"But where are we going?"

"There!" He nodded toward a prospect hole, one of the many that had been dug in these mountains by miners. As soon as he had heard the blooper cough its interrupted rocket blast when it changed direction in the sky, he had instantly looked for a hiding place. This tunnel seemed to fill the bill.

"Is something going to happen?" the nurse asked.

"In less than two minutes you will find out," he answered. His long legs had already started taking him toward the hole. After hesitating for an instant, the nurse hastily followed him.

The prospect hole extended less than ten feet into the side of the mountain and was not timbered. This was good. It meant no heavy beams would collapse around their heads when the hills began to shake. A quick examination revealed that the stone of the roof seemed to be solid. Zen stopped within three feet of the entrance.

"Why don't we go farther back?" the nurse asked.

"We're in far enough for protection from bits of flying metal but not too far to dig ourselves out if the roof should collapse—I hope," Zen answered.

Somewhere outside a man screamed, in terror.

The thing in the sky coughed again, closer now. BRRROOOM-MM——BrrroooMMM——BrOOOm!

The blooper struck.

The sound was that of the simultaneous firing of many cannon. The walls of the prospect tunnel seemed to twist and wave. Loose stones dropped from the roof and a fine dust seemed to extrude from the walls. A boulder half as big as a small house hurtled past the entrance, snapping pines like matchsticks. A slide of loose rocks followed it. In the distance another slide could be heard growling back at the sky as it grew to avalanche proportions.

The nurse's fingers tightened on Zen's arm, then relaxed. Every nerve in his body was as taut as a steel wire as he waited for her reaction. Other than the tightening and relaxing of her fingers, there was none. Her hands remained on his arm and she remained in the tunnel with him. To Kurt Zen, this was disappointing.

"What kind of nerves do you have? Most women would have been in my arms and would have had their noses buried in my chest."

"I'm sorry, colonel, if my education in how to be afraid has been neglected." She coughed at the dust.

"Aren't you really afraid, Nedra?" he asked.

"No."

"Then you aren't an ordinary human!" The instant he had blurted out the words, he was sorry he had spoken. It was possible to give away too much too soon.

"Then what am I?" Her voice was calm.

He dodged her question. "Aren't you even afraid to die?"

"When so many have died already, why should I hesitate to join them?" the nurse answered. She released his arm and brushed dust from the shoulders of her uniform. She glanced up at him and it seemed that some kind of a radiation flowed from her eyes, a wave of it that sent a tingle over his entire skin surface. Outside, another smaller boulder went bouncing past the entrance to the tunnel. Fumbling in his pockets for cigarettes, Zen found a crumpled package. He offered one to the nurse but she thanked him and refused it. He did not insist. Cigarettes were too precious to waste on people who didn't really want them. Outside, another man began to scream. The nurse moved automatically in that direction. He caught her arm and held her back.

"Wait until the rocks stop rolling, Nedra."

She did not protest. Looking up at him, she said, "You think I'm one of the new people, don't you?"

Zen coughed and swore at the cigarette, insisting that the tobacco was moist. This was a lie and both knew it. But—what to say? Her question was a complete stunner. "What makes you think that?" he asked, desperate for words.

"I just think it. It's true, isn't it?"

As an intelligence officer, Zen was accustomed to asking the questions, but this nurse had completely turned the tables on him. He took a deep drag on the cigarette. "I don't know. Are you?" He made his voice as casual as was possible.

Her eyes studied him. The trace of a smile came over her face and tugged at the corners of her lips. "Do you mind if I ask you a question?"

"Go right ahead." The man had stopped screaming outside but another boulder was going past. In the distance, the avalanche was trying to grind to a halt but it sounded as if millions of tons of rock were on the move to a safer location.

"Are *you* one of the new people?" the nurse asked.

The cough was real this time. Zen could not suppress his surprise. "What on earth makes you ask a question like that?"

"I just felt like asking it," the nurse replied. "Am I wrong?"

"Who are the new people?"

"Why, everybody has heard of them. They're the new race that is going to provide the nucleus for new growth after all ordinary men and women have been destroyed in this war." Surprise showed in her violet eyes. "Do you mean you have never heard of them?"

"I've heard the usual rumors that are afloat," Zen said, shrugging. "But all the stories have impressed me as a pack of lies. Really, I think the enemy has started most of them, to get us to relax our war effort."

"Do you honestly think that?" Her voice had a puzzled note in it. "I mean, honestly and truly."

"I think what the evidence tells me to think, nothing less. In this case, I have seen none of the so-called evidence."

Shrugging, Zen moved toward the opening of the tunnel, then drew back as a mass of rock crashed outside. "It's raining boulders out there," he said. "What do you know about the so-called new people?"

"Not much," she answered.

"You're a very lovely liar, but the fact that you are lovely doesn't make you any less a liar," Zen said. She was very beautiful with her violet eyes and bronze hair, but an overworked intelligence officer could not be concerned with these things.

"Thank you, colonel," she said. "But I do not relish being called a liar." Her face showed hurt, just the right amount of it, but at the same time her eyes laughed at him. "However, I guess there is nothing I can do about it, is there?" Somehow she contrived to look like a small girl who has been unjustly accused of some deed she has not committed.

In the distance the avalanche had ground to a halt. Now, no more boulders were bounding down the hill. A vast, puzzled silence held the mountains. In that silence, Zen fancied he could hear the thoughts of the frightened men who had remained alive thus far, and were wondering how to prolong their precarious existence. They were also wondering if staying alive was worth the effort involved. Why not give up now and be done with all tragedy, with all tears, with all trying to find the road to the future?

Up the trail a man began to scream.

Like a homing pigeon that has finally found the right direction, the nurse moved toward the sound. Zen caught her arm again. Looking puzzled, she stopped. "Please, colonel. I am needed up there." She nodded up the slope in the direction of the screaming man.

"You are probably needed by many others," he commented.

She did not seem to understand. "But I am a nurse. It is my duty to help those who are wounded."

"I know." He was a little startled to find himself in sympathy with this impulse. "But, not yet."

"Why not?"

"Because that slope is still too hot to be safe." He held up his left wrist. Instead of a watch, he wore a miniature radiation counter there. The needle was creeping up toward the red line.

"The radiation count is about forty right here at the mouth of this prospect hole," he pointed out.

"That is interesting," the nurse said. The tone of her voice said it was not important.

"Halfway up the slope, it will hit a hundred. At the top of the ridge, where the explosion took place, the count may reach a thousand." In his opinion, he had said enough.

In her opinion, he had not said anything at all. "That makes no difference. Wounded men are up there. I am a nurse. My duty is clear to me."

"If you try to help them under these circumstances, you will become a casualty yourself."

"But what of the men who need help?"

"They will simply have to get out of the radiation zone themselves, or wait until the area is clear and help can reach them."

"You are heartless!"

"Not at all," he denied. "If anything could be done to help them I would be doing it. Don't you understand what has happened? That was an Asian N bomb that exploded. In an N bomb the immediate effect is minor. The real purpose of the weapon is to spray the area with high intensity radiation, to make the ground unfit for living for months. Any living creature caught within the direct blast of the radiation is doomed, and neither you, nor I, nor the medics, can do anything to help them—" He broke off as another man began screaming up the slope.

The nurse was irresolute. "But that man needs help," she pointed out.

"Certainly he needs help," Zen agreed.

"Well—"

Zen watched her carefully. She seemed to understand his words but something else pulled at her far more strongly: the screaming of the injured man. Each time the soldier cried out, she started in his direction.

"Well, well, thank you, colonel." Turning, she moved with a sure stride up the slope.

Zen swore under his breath and started after her, then caught the motion as the question rose in him as to why she should throw her life away. She knew the meaning of radiation in lethal quantities. Unquestionably, she also knew what would happen to any normal human who ventured into a hot zone.

Was she, then, a normal human being? Was he actually witnessing one of the miracles performed by the new people? If she came off the mountain slope alive, it would certainly prove something. Zen cursed again. She was going where he could not safely follow. If she returned unharmed, he had enough proof to warrant following her to the ends of the earth, if need be.

CHAPTER III

The radio transmitter inside Zen's pack was small but very powerful. It did not look like a radio transmitter at all; there was no antenna and no apparent source of power. Only the tiny earphone and the throat microphone revealed its true nature.

He slipped the phone into his ear, fitted the microphone against his throat, then picked up the piece of plastic tubing that was red on one end and green on the other. Wires ran from each end of this tube to the small box that housed the transmitter.

"Red goes to the right hand," he muttered. "Green to the left. Or is it the other way around?" Making up his mind that red went to the right, he closed his fingers around the ends of the plastic tube, then watched the tiny meter on top of the small box that contained the transmitter.

The needle moved on the dial.

"Calling nine dash nine," he spoke. "This is six one calling nine dash nine." He repeated the call three times, then sat back on his haunches to await an answer.

"Come in six one," the earphone said. "What color is red?"

"It's green this week," Zen answered promptly.

"What color was it last week?"

"Last week? Um. Oh, yes. No color."

"And that means—"

"White. This is Kurt Zen, colonel, intelligence, reporting. Connect me immediately with General Stocker."

Satisfied with the identity of the caller, the operator said, "Just a minute, colonel, I'll see if the general will talk to you."

"Tell him it's important," Zen urged.

"They always say that," the operator sighed. "I'll put you through as soon as I can."

"Kurt, boy, where are you?" General Stocker's voice boomed into a distant microphone. The general's voice always boomed, he was always hearty, he was always sure that while things might look black right now, they would work out all right in the end. By the time the booming voice reached Zen's earphone, it had been transformed into a tinny squeak. Kurt thought he detected an uneasy note in the squeak and he wondered if the general had finally glimpsed the end, and was finding it not quite as he had supposed.

"In hell, general," Zen answered. He swiftly told where he was and what had happened. "Cuso's blooper knocked out the last pass by which we can bring an effective force against him. This whole area is loaded with radiation."

"How will we ever root that bastard out of his hole now?"

"That's for the staff to decide. I have more important news."

"Yes? Talk, Kurt, and fast. You don't mean that you—"

"Yes. I mean I think this nurse may be it. I don't know yet." Zen explained what had happened.

"Damn it, Kurt, do you mean to tell me that if she comes back alive, you will know she is immune to the radiation, and hence must be one of the new people? But if she comes back dead, or so loaded with radiation that she will die within a few days, then you will know she was just like all the rest of us?" Even through Zen's earphone, the general's voice had begun to boom.

"That's the way I see it," Zen answered.

"But goddammit—Are you hurt, Kurt?" The general's voice was suddenly solicitous. "Are you all right?"

"Damn it, I'm in my right mind," Zen answered. "I was in a prospect hole when the blast went off. Don't you think I've got enough sense to take cover?" Stocker's suddenly solicitous attitude irritated him. "Sorry, sir," he apologized an instant later.

"It's quite all right, boy. I know that nerves get frayed in combat. But this nurse—"

"That's the way I see it, sir," Zen said doggedly. "I request permission to follow her."

"If she comes back alive, you mean?"

"I would appreciate it if you would stop reminding me of that possibility."

"Oh. So you are emotionally interested in her?"

"Well, what if I am? She's a nice kid."

"They all are, boy. They all are—until you get to know them. As to permission to follow her, you've not only got it, but it's an order. We've got to find out about these new people. One of them appeared in President Wilkerson's private office this morning and told him to call off a planned landing in Asia."

"Really?" Zen said. "In the President's office!"

"That's what I said."

"Did it really happen? I mean, was anyone present?"

"No one except the President's secretary. She's under heavy sedation right now, from shock. She thought God Almighty Himself had come walking in. The old man is not in much better shape." Stocker's voice showed signs of strain. "I've got my orders from Wilkerson himself and I'm passing them on to you. *Find these new people!* Follow that nurse to hell if you have to."

"Right, sir."

"Report to me when you have something to report—that is, something besides going to bed with her. Off." Zen grimaced as he pulled the tiny phone out of his ear. He slipped the transmitter back into the pack and slung it over his shoulder. The radiation count was dropping but it was still too high for safety. He looked longingly up the trail. Wounded men were coming down but Nedra was not in sight.

The wounded men were no longer a fighting unit, but had become individuals, each one intent only on his own survival. Patriotism had gone from their minds, they no longer gave a hoot about saving their country, but were only interested in saving their own lives.

Far up the trail, Zen could see a tall figure moving upward. The nurse! He unslung the pair of field glasses from his shoulder. Through the powerful lenses Nedra's lithe figure was very clear. He saw her move to the side of the trail and kneel beside a wounded man who lacked the courage to walk downhill. Somehow she got the man to his feet and started him along the trail. He stumbled and fell. Again the nurse knelt beside him but this time she made no attempt to lift him. Instead, she got to her own feet.

Zen decided the man had died as he fell.

She continued on up the slope.

Down below, motors roared and then came to a halt. Turning, Zen saw that a first aid station was being set up down there. The medics worked fast; already they were directing the wounded men to the back end of a truck, where an examination station had been set up. But, fast as they worked, they were too late to help the vast majority of the wounded. The futility of the effort depressed Zen, so he returned his attention to the nurse.

She was in the middle of the trail again. The avalanche, directly ahead of her, had stopped her progress. A man was with her.

Through the glasses, the man looked as tall and craggy as a mountain peak. No soldier, he was without helmet or other headgear. His hair, white as the snow on top of a mountain, was flying in the wind. His face looked like a statue hewn in granite. Zen guessed that he was a resident of this region, a mountaineer who had sought safety in these remote fastnesses, and who had been blasted out of his hiding place by Cuso's radioactive blooper and was wandering down this trail to die. The nurse was talking to him.

Involuntarily, as if they had a will of their own, Zen's legs started carrying him up the slope. He had taken a dozen steps before he remembered the counter on his wrist.

"To hell with the count!" he thought. "I'm going up there and drag her down here. She's not going to throw her life away while I skulk like a coward down below. I don't give a damn whether she's one of the new people or not. She's human!"

He climbed the slope with giant strides. Then he saw that Nedra was running toward him and waving him back.

"Colonel! You can't come up here."

"I *am* coming up there!" he shouted in reply.

"No!"

When he did not stop, she ran faster toward him. The craggy man kept pace with her. Reaching Zen, she caught his sleeve, turned him around, and started him down the slope. "You can't be here." Her voice was breathless with protest.

"Are you giving me orders?" Zen growled. Secretly he was pleased because she was concerned about him.

"If you will permit me, colonel, I think Nedra's intention is to save your life," the craggy man spoke. He had a voice like a bell tolling in the distance, sweet-toned and musical, but with overtones of great strength.

"What about *her* life?" Zen demanded.

"I'm going down now, colonel," the nurse said hastily. "They've set up a first aid station. They will need me there."

"You will need their attention is what you mean," Zen said.

"Colonel, the counter!" she answered.

The needle was well over the hundred mark and was still rising.

"Come, colonel." Hooking her arm in his, Nedra began moving down the rough, boulder-strewn trail. Zen did not move. She tugged harder.

"Your life is in danger here, sir," the craggy man said, politely.

"That is of interest to me only," Zen answered. "And what about your life?"

"Colonel, I'd like you to meet a friend of mine," the nurse said quickly. "Colonel Zen, Sam West. We'll talk while we walk down to the first aid station."

"A pleasure to meet you, sir," West said, extending his hand. His handclasp was firm but there was a suggestion of additional power in his fingers.

"Nice to meet you, Mr. West. Do you live around here?"

"Over that way," the craggy man said, nodding vaguely over his shoulder.

Again the nurse tugged at Zen's arm. He set his feet solidly on the mountain trail. "We'll talk right here."

"But you are taking an unfair advantage of Nedra," the craggy man protested. "This area is heavy with radiation and this is neither the time nor the place to be swapping horses."

"Then why are you two here?"

"I was getting out of the area as fast as I could when I met Nedra," West said. "I would still be getting out of it, but fast, if you were not stopping me."

"I'm not stopping you," Zen said. "There's the trail. Hit it. Nor you either," he said to Nedra.

"Don't be silly, Kurt," the nurse said. She was pleading with him now.

"All right. But on one condition. Why did you come up here in the first place? You knew the area was hot."

"I—I lost my head," the nurse said promptly. "My emotions ran away with me. I'm a nurse and wounded men needed my attention. I went to them. You will come down the trail with us, won't you?" The violet eyes begged him to believe in her.

"What made you lose your head?"

"Why—shock, I suppose. This is the first time I was bombed. Also, the screaming of the wounded. Really, sir, I am a nurse." The way she said the word, being a nurse meant something. The violet eyes had grown tired of begging and were on the verge of spitting anger at him.

"I don't believe a damned word you have said," Zen said. "You didn't lose your head back there in the prospect hole."

"Please, Kurt." Again she rugged at his arm. "I'll talk to you all you want down below. But don't try to force me to stay here."

Reluctantly, Zen yielded to the pressure on his arm. Relief appeared in the violet eyes and the face of the craggy man showed a sudden release from some inner strain. Dimly, he thought he had seen that craggy face somewhere before but the picture that flicked through his mind was gone before he could fit a time and place tag on it. Going down the trail, he steered the nurse toward a truck where the medics had set up equipment to test the amount of exposure to radiation. In doing this, he discovered that she was steering him in the same direction.

"I don't need the medics," he protested. "I'm all right. I wasn't exposed long enough to do any damage."

"Of course you're all right," she answered. Her tone was similar to that of an indulgent mother reassuring a hurt child.

"You're the one who needs help," he said. He was certain she had remained too long.

"I'm going to get it if I need it," she said, soothingly.

Zen could hear the occasional crunch of boots behind them. West was keeping silent. He did not seem to be in a hurry.

Zen started to speak to Nedra. The thought of what he wanted to say was dim in his mind and he could not quite find words for it but he knew that it had something to do with a wish that the world were different and that the human race were not trying to destroy itself. Why should he be wishing this? The reason for his thinking became a little clearer. He was wishing the world were different so that he might make love to this nurse under conditions that would permit this love to bear other fruit than frustration, despair, and death.

He found himself wishing that a vine-covered cottage existed somewhere, a place where a man and a woman might live in peace and reasonable security, raising some kids who could play on a mountain slope that was not saturated with atomic radiation.

"Here is the first aid station," the nurse said. "And—"

"And what?" he asked her when she did not continue.

She gave his arm a squeeze. "And thank you for the dream," she whispered.

As Kurt Zen turned startled eyes toward her, wondering how she had known what he had been dreaming, her face seemed to dissolve in a gray mist.

He plunged, unconscious, to the ground at her feet.

CHAPTER IV

The jar of striking the ground seemed to bring the intelligence agent back to consciousness instantly. As Nedra started to kneel beside him, he was already getting to his feet. She tried to help him rise. He shrugged her hand away.

"What happened?" she asked.

"Nothing," he said. This didn't seem quite right. "I—I—" He tried to think what had happened. "I fainted. That's all. I just fainted." To him, this seemed a reasonable explanation for everything that needed explaining.

Nedra seemed to think otherwise. "But men like you don't just faint," she protested.

"I did."

"They don't faint unless something is wrong with them," Nedra continued. "Are you sure you're not suffering from delayed shock following the bomb explosion? Or—" Her voice slid away into silence as if she were afraid to voice the thought that was in her mind. Behind her, West said nothing.

"I just did it," Zen said, becoming more indignant. "I fainted. Who says it can't be done?" Confusion existed somewhere. He was sure it was the nurse who was confused. He shook his head in an effort to clear up her difficulty.

"I saw you do it. All I am trying to say is that perhaps there may be a reason for it."

"Nope," Zen said. "I'm not going to the aid station. No reason for it. I'm all right. It's the world out there that is wrong." This made sense to him.

"I know you are all right," Nedra answered. Her face showed strain. "But it might be a good idea to have the doctors check, just to make sure."

Zen, busy shaking his head again, hardly heard her. He had the impression that her confusion would clear up in a minute. Somehow it reminded him of the confusion that he had suffered after inhaling a whiff of nerve gas, once. When had this happened? He was not sure, now.

Perhaps it had taken place in the remote past, perhaps on some other planet ... he realized his mind was wandering. Again he shook his head.

"But I really think, colonel—"

"I wasn't shaking my head at you," Zen corrected.

"Good. Then we will go see the doctors."

"I didn't mean that either. I was shaking my head to clear it. There's a fog in it."

"A fog in your head?" Unease appeared in her voice.

"Yes. What's wrong with that? Lots of men have fogs in their heads." To him, this seemed a reasonable statement. "Lots of men have to go to the docs every couple of weeks to have the fogs blown out of their heads." Thinking he had made a joke, he laughed.

Nedra did not think he had said anything funny. Resolutely, she took his arm. "Come with me, colonel." As she led him toward the truck which the medics were using for a first aid station, something happened.

He saw clearly.

He saw everything.

The ability to see came suddenly, out of nowhere. One second it was not there. Then it was there. It was like seeing with eyes, except it was better than ocular perception had ever been. With it, he was not only able to see surfaces, he could also see into the interior of things. An acute understanding of what he saw went with the perception.

He saw that the Universe was as tall as a man, and no taller. He saw that it was as wide as a man, and no wider. He saw that it was as broad as a man, and no broader.

He saw the human race in its entirety, one man and all men, all men in one man. Simultaneously, he saw the whole history of the race, he saw the long journey it had made from so-called inanimate matter to the point where it was now a creature that looked outward to the stars. He saw that the destiny of the race lay in those stars, and in all that vast expanse of space between them, if it did not destroy itself in the process of growing to star stature. He saw that the race could do exactly this, that it could blow itself back to the component atoms that composed it, in which case the long and toilsome, heart-breaking struggle upward from the atomic level would have to begin all over again.

He also knew what he was doing with this clear seeing.

He was touching the race mind.

He was in contact with the race field.

His consciousness had been lifted to the level of that vast, all-pervading, but very subtle force field that comprised the race mind.

The knowledge was sudden agony in him, a pain that was needle sharp in the region of his heart. The pain was strange because, while he could feel it and knew it was happening in his body, it had no meaning to him. He was detached from it, it hurt his body, but it did not hurt or harm him.

His body was alarmed by the pain, his breathing quickened, and a faint trace of sweat appeared on his skin. But he was not alarmed. Even if his body fell dead, he would not be concerned.

"What is it, Kurt?" his ears heard Nedra say. She had detected his heavy breathing and she was alarmed. "Are you about to faint again?"

"No," his lips answered. His body laughed at the question. He heard the sound of his laughter as being both his and not his. His body knew it was not going to faint. His laughter sounded hollow and out of place but he did not care about that either.

Ahead, soldiers were lined up at the back end of the truck, waiting their turn in line.

"Your rank entitles you to priority," Nedra said hesitantly.

"In the place where I am now, my rank doesn't exist," he answered. "I join the end of the line, I take my turn." He was quite stubborn about this.

The nurse looked pleased. He wondered if he had said something important. To him, what he had said seemed obvious. Behind him, West was a silent shadow wrapped in an enigma. Even with his sudden new perception, his contact with a higher form of consciousness, he could not perceive West clearly. Something about the craggy man defied penetration and analysis.

The men in the line ahead of him waited for their turn, shuffling forward each time the medics finished with their examination. There was no talk in the line. Not a man grumbled, not a man complained. Knowing men, Zen knew that this was ominous.

These men had had it. They knew they had had it. In the face of that knowledge, nothing else mattered. Outwardly, they looked fit. Inwardly, something had happened to them. It seemed to Zen that he could see glows coming from their bodies. One was swaying. Zen seemed to glimpse a blob of light moving suddenly upward from the man. The soldier fell. He did not move a muscle after he hit.

Nedra started toward him. Zen shook his head. "No use," he said.
"Why not?"
Zen pointed skyward. "He went that way."
Her face whitened as she caught his meaning. "I'll make sure."
She moved forward and inspected the fallen man, felt for a pulse, and felt again, then got to her feet. As she returned, her back seemed to have acquired a new sag.

An officer shouted from the truck, his voice gravel rough from tension. In response, a stretcher-bearing detail moved forward. They inspected the body of the fallen man, then lifted it and tossed it to the side of the trail. One clipped a dog tag from it, then ran a counter over it, He grunted to his companion, who tied a red tag on the dead man's wrist.

"Up that way, boys, you can find some more," Zen called to them, jerking his thumb up the slope.

"We're not a burial detail," was the answer.

The soldiers in the line shuffled forward.

"Hey! It's gone!" Zen said suddenly.

"What's gone?"

"I'm back," Zen said.

"You never went anywhere," the nurse said.

"*It's gone* and *I'm back* both mean the same thing," he tried to explain. "The thing that is gone is my contact with the race field. *I'm back* means that all of a sudden, I'm normal. I'm back here. I'm looking out of my eyes. I'm hearing with my ears. I don't know everything any longer."

Daze was in him. Worse than the daze was the fact that even the memory of the experience was receding. Agony came with this recession. It seemed to him that this experience was the most important thing that had ever happened to him.

And it was going away. He watched it slide out of his memory. He felt like running wildly to try and recapture it. Which way he would run did not matter, just so he ran until he found it again. He fought the impulse to run. The experience was not out there; it could not be found if he searched the whole world for it.

It was inside him.

Nedra looked at West and started to speak, but the craggy man motioned her to silence.

"Saul on the road to Damascus," Zen muttered. "Something like this happened to Saul on the road to Damascus."

"Kurt—" Nedra said. Again the craggy man motioned her to silence. The fellow, rough mountaineer that he was, seemed to have some perception of the turmoil inside a fellow human being, and more than that, to have understanding and sympathy.

"I contacted the race mind," Zen said. "For a minute, I was in touch with the field of the race. But it's gone now," he added. Sadness and a falling voice went with the last words.

"Step in front of the scope, soldier," a gravel voice growled behind him. Turning, he saw that he was next in line. The lieutenant in charge of the first aid station had spoken to him. Seeing the eagle on Zen's helmet he hastily apologized. "I beg your pardon, sir."

"It's all right," Zen said. For an instant, as conflicting ideas competed for expression in him, he wondered who he was and why he was here. Then he remembered what had happened. Well established reaction patterns took over and he stepped into position in front of the scope. Inside the back end of the truck, a transformer hummed. Although he could not feel it, he knew that a powerful stream of radiation was passing through his body and that a count was being made of the radioactivity he had absorbed. The lieutenant studied his meters, then looked up at Zen.

"You're all right, sir." He seemed puzzled.

"Not hot, eh?"

"No, sir, you're not. Frankly, I don't understand it. Oh, you've got a little exposure, but nothing serious."

"I was in one of the old mines when the blast went off," Zen explained.

"Then that accounts for it. You were lucky as hell, sir. Next."

Catching Nedra's arm, Zen swung her in front of the scope. The experience with higher levels of consciousness had been forced out of his mind, and he was all intelligence officer.

"But I'm all right! I mean, there's nothing wrong. Are you out of your mind again?"

"Yes," Zen said. "But I've got the rank to make my decisions stick whether I'm out of my mind or not. Lieutenant, check this woman. This is an order!" Zen snapped out the words with all the precision and authority of a drill-field sergeant training recruits.

"Yes, sir," the startled medical officer said.

Ignoring Nedra's protests, Zen held her in place while the equipment was put into operation. Behind them, West watched. The faintest trace of an approving smile showed on the craggy man's face.

The lieutenant looked up from his meters. "She's all right too, sir."

"Sure of that?"

"Of course I'm sure. This counter doesn't lie!" The medical officer was indignant.

So was Nedra. The violet eyes shot sparks of anger at the colonel. Zen was unimpressed. Deep inside, he was tremendously relieved. She had come down alive! She was unharmed! This was enough to make him feel good all over. He also knew what she was. No ordinary mortal could have remained in the hot zone for the length of time she had been there and emerged unharmed. He did not mind her anger. Instead he turned to West.

"You're next!"

He did not know what response to expect from the craggy man. It might be anything. To his surprise, West smiled.

"Glad to, colonel. I was hoping I would get tested, so I would know where I stood."

Without hesitation, West stepped in front of the scope. "While I am certain I did not receive enough exposure to do any damage, still it is best to follow your example and make certain " The deep voice was suave, with tiny overtones of amusement in it somewhere.

Again the lieutenant studied his meters and again he looked up. Real perplexity was on his face. "Three okays in a row. I didn't have a single okay up until now." His gaze went up the slope in the direction where the bomb had exploded.

"Does that mean I'm all right?" West asked.

"Yes. Definitely all right," the lieutenant answered. "And I don't pretend to understand it."

"I was in a hole, too," West said. He seemed to be amused at some joke known only to him.

The lieutenant brightened. "Then I understand it."

"I wish I did," Zen said, to himself. There was no longer any doubt in his mind that Nedra was one of the new people. As to West, the man was an enigma. Not knowing how long West had been exposed to the radiation, Zen did not know what to make of his freedom from it. But there was certainly something peculiar about him.

"Colonel, it was good to meet you." West was coming toward him with outstretched hand. Zen had the impression that the man's hand could turn into a veritable bear trap, if West chose. "Perhaps we shall meet again, sir." The words were a statement, not a question. An enigmatical smile played over the craggy man's face.

"Who knows whether we shall meet again?" Zen answered, shrugging. "Generally, when people say goodbye these days, they mean goodbye forever."

"I know." Sadness showed on the craggy, lined face. "It is too bad that things have to be this way. Well, experience is a difficult school, but *homo sapiens* seems incapable of learning in any other."

"It is war," Zen said.

"I disagree with you there," West said. "War is only a symptom of the disease, it is only an expression of humanity. War itself is not at fault, but man. Nor can man really be regarded as being at fault, since what he is now going through is only a stage of growth."

Momentarily the memory of the contact with the race mind flicked through Zen's consciousness. "I know that," he said. Then he hesitated. "Or I knew it once."

"Ah? When?"

"Up the slope there, I knew it. But I have forgotten now what I knew." Zen spoke slowly. He was trying hard to remember—or to forget—he wasn't sure which.

"Ah?" West repeated. "Goodday, sir. Nedra, I would like to speak with you for a moment, before I leave. With your permission, of course, Colonel Zen."

"Certainly," Zen said. He watched the nurse and the craggy man move up the trail a few steps. They carried on a conversation in tones too low for him to overhear, then parted. West went down to the bottom of the ravine and crossed to the other side of the gulch, where he began to climb the opposite slope, staying as far away from the radioactive zone as possible. Nedra returned to Zen beside the truck.

"Does he live back there?" the intelligence agent asked.

"I really don't know," the nurse answered. "I think he does, but I'm not certain."

"It's rough country to live in."

"From what I have seen of him, he seems capable of living almost anywhere."

"Do you know him well?"

The violet eyes regarded him thoughtfully. "You are asking a great many questions, sir."

"I'm going to ask more."

"My telephone number, no doubt. I'm sorry, but I don't have a telephone." The violet eyes grew pensive. "But if I did have a telephone number, there is no one I would rather give it to than you."

He felt a warm glow at her words. The dream that he had once shared with millions of other men, of a wife and kids, came into his mind again, a yearning that was as old as history. If he had his free choice, he would go with this dream.

He knew he did not have a free choice. Indeed, he doubted if he had any choice at all. Nor had any other man. History had moved past the day when this dream could be realized. Fate was sweeping it into the dust heap of good things that were gone forever.

CHAPTER V

"She is immune to radiation!" Zen thought after Nedra had left to rejoin her unit. This in itself was of sufficient importance to attract and hold the interest of the top military and scientific minds. Perhaps soldiers could also be immunized. Perhaps, by some impossible freak of chance, a way might be found for workers to return to abandoned factories, to long-closed shops and forges. This might mean a new flow of goods and materials to troops that were desperately short of them and to a civilian population that, at a conservative estimate, was more than half starved.

A human being who had achieved immunity to radiation was important enough to command his complete attention. Also, the probability was very great that she was one of the mysterious new people. Something else about her interested him even more. He could not put his finger on this something else but he suspected it had to do with the future, with another world than the one he knew. Or with another universe. Again the memory of his contact with the race mind flicked through his consciousness.

Now he knew what he was going to do insofar as Nedra was concerned. He had a hunch what her next move would be. He would wait for her to make it.

Finding a carbine was not difficult. On this trail, the weapons were to be had for picking them up. A dead man's ammunition pouches were filled with cartridges. He took the pouches. Carrying the carbine, he slid down the bank toward the mountain stream that talked to itself at the bottom of the canyon. The water was clear and cool but dead trout floating in it warned him not to drink.

Seeking a place from which he could watch the canyon, he moved upward. A dim trail was visible through the pines here.

"An old narrow-gauge railroad," he thought. The rails had been removed long since, the ties had rotted away, and the roadbed itself was hardly a trail through the growth of trees. He had barely settled himself in a spot from which to watch the ravine below, than a stone turned on the old roadbed.

Nedra was coming along the trail.

He let her pass without challenge. Sliding out of hiding, he followed her.

Twisting and turning, the trail climbed slowly upward. When it reached the edge of the timber, Zen caught a glimpse of a slide of yellow rock far ahead, an old mine dump, which told him why the road had been constructed in the first place. A ghost town was probably ahead.

He caught a glimpse of Nedra moving steadily ahead along the old road bed.

"If she doesn't know exactly where she is going, then I'm missing my guess," he thought, as he followed her. Elation was rising in him. She was leading him straight to the hiding place of the new people.

Here in these mountains a small group could remain in hiding forever. Food might eventually become a problem, but there was plenty of game in the ranges: deer, elk, and bear, and some of the high valleys had been in cultivation before the war. A few hardy pioneers had always managed to find a living in this wilderness. If they could do it, so could this new group.

Of course, they would have to evade Cuso's roving patrols, raiding for food, supplies and women. But that ought not to be too difficult. The ghost town was in sight.

Surrounding an old mine, a crusher, and a concentrator, the ghost town was also in ruins. Unlike so many small cities, the ruin here had not come from attack but from nature. The snows of winter had piled their burden on flimsy roofs, the seepage of spring had rotted the timbers, with the result that many of the houses had simply collapsed. Weeds grew in the doorways and scrub cedars had found roots in the streets.

Nedra was walking down the middle of what had once been the main street. Her stride was still certain and she seemed to know exactly where she was going.

The ragged man appeared in the door of the garage on her left. He spoke to the nurse, calling to her. She jumped at the sound of the voice, glanced at the man, then continued walking.

"Hey, wait a minute, cutie!" the fellow shouted, loud enough for Zen to hear him. He lunged out of the doorway toward her. She turned to face him.

Kurt Zen lifted the carbine, then dropped the muzzle. He not only had great confidence in Nedra's ability to protect herself, but he wanted to see what would happen.

The loop of rope, thrown with all the skill of a cowboy, came from the opposite side of the street. It settled over her shoulders, pinned her arms to the side, and was instantly jerked tight. She was pulled to the ground.

The man who had lunged out of the doorway of the garage leaped toward her. Throwing her on her stomach, face down, he jerked both hands behind her back, then began to search her for a weapon.

The man who had thrown the rope came out of hiding to help his companion. He was short, with bow legs.

Together, they held the nurse down.

Zen raised the carbine to his shoulders. Although he had not previously fired this weapon, at this distance he could not miss.

Her scream came to his ears.

"Colonel! Watch out!"

In startled surprise, he slid the carbine from his shoulder. She had known he was following her and that he was somewhere near! Thoughts like startled hornets flicked through his consciousness. How had she known he was following her? Why had she let him do it? More important, where was she leading him? Most important of all, why was she trying to save him when her own life was in danger?

Even if she had known he was following her, obviously she hadn't known these men were here. She hadn't been coming to meet them. Then what was her purpose in climbing to this old ghost town which lay just at timberline on the edge of a mountain wilderness where Cuso was held at bay?

The first ruffian was standing erect. Zen brought the sights of the carbine to bear on the center of his ragged coat.

"*Drop the gun!*" a voice said behind him.

Even more surprising than the command was the fact that he knew the voice that had spoken. Or he thought he did. He let the carbine slide from his fingers.

"Now get 'em up."

He raised his hands. "Hello, Jake," he called out.

An exclamation of surprise came from behind him. "How the hell did you know me?"

"Recognized your voice," Zen answered. "Can I turn around now?"

"Sure. Sure. But what the hell are you doing up here?"

Turning, Zen saw the automatic rifle that covered him. The muzzle was wavering and the man who held it seemed confused. His face was covered with a heavy growth of black whiskers and long hair peeped out from under a battered helmet.

"Jake, it's really good to see you again." As if such things as automatic rifles did not exist, Zen advanced with outstretched hand.

"Kurt Zen! I haven't seen you since—since—"

"The night that Denver got it," Zen answered. Horror overwhelmed him as he remembered what had happened to the Mile-High city. A bomb had struck from the sky that night and parts of Denver had gone much higher than a mile.

"Yeah. That's it. Yeah. I thought you had got it that night, Kurt."

"I thought the same thing about you. What are you doing up here? And what—what happened to Marcia?"

The instant Zen asked the question, he wished he had kept still. At the name something happened in the man's eyes. They began to change, going from comprehension to blankness, then coming back to understanding, then losing that and going back to blankness. One instant the eyes looked at Zen and the man remembered and liked this colonel. The next instant, neither the eyes nor the mind behind them knew him. Zen was then an alien, a stranger, to be distrusted and feared and possibly destroyed. When Zen had known him in Denver, Jake had been a young airman. He and Marcia had been newly married and very much in love with each other.

"She—she—" The voice was choked and tight with pain. "The radiation got her." For an instant, the memory held true. But there was too much pain in the memory for this man to face it. The memory went away. Only the pain remained. "Marcia? Oh, she's fine. The next leave I get, we're going to have a second honeymoon." A glow appeared in the man's eyes. "I can see her now, waiting for me. You must go with me, Kurt, and meet her again, the next leave I get."

Zen could have slugged him. He could have lifted the rifle out of Jake's hands without protest. Instead, he did nothing. The man's pain was much too real to hurt him further.

"What's going on here?" a rough voice said.

It was the man in the ragged coat. Nedra and the man who had thrown the rope had disappeared. There was no indication where they had gone. This man's beard was thin and ragged. He had teeth like the fangs of a wolf but the lights in his eyes did not shift. Instead, they remained fixed in constant hostility and suspicion. He had a sub-machine gun in his hands. The muzzle covered Zen.

"Oh, hello, Cal. I—" Jake became confused. "This is an old buddy of mine. I knew him down below ... I knew him when.... He's all right."

Cal's eyes said he did not believe a word he had heard. He looked Zen up and down. The muzzle of the gun did not waver from the intelligence agent's stomach. "What are you doing up here?"

"Maybe I got tired of the way things are down there," Zen answered. He was not lying. He *was* tired of the way things were going. So were uncounted millions of others.

Cal's eyes indicated he did not believe this. Zen could see him turning over different possibilities in his mind. He was inclined to use the gun. Dumping another body down the gorge would be an easy solution to the problem of an intruder. "How are things going down there?" he asked.

"Tough," Zen said, with conviction in his voice.

"What was the big boom over that way this morning?"

"Cuso letting go with a blooper."

Interest kindled in Cal's eyes. "What was over there that was worth the cost of a blooper?"

"A column of troops heading for Cuso's lair," Zen answered. "He didn't like it."

"I guess he wouldn't," Cal said. "You with 'em?"

"I was."

"Which way are they going now?"

"Back down hill to die," Zen answered.

"Why didn't you go with 'em?"

"I got tired," Zen said. He waved his hands in a gesture which was intended to explain how a man sometimes got tired and went off to rest for a while. Cal grunted. This he understood.

"Are you hot?" he asked.

"Nope. The medics checked me just before I took off."

"And are there others down there who feel like heading for the hills?"

"Most of them are too damned near dead to make the effort. Why desert when you've had it?"

"The blooper got a lot of 'em, eh?"

"What the blast didn't get, the radioactivity did."

"Is the pass too hot for more troops to go through it?"

"My guess is that way."

"Your guess? Don't you know?"

"I didn't go up to see. I'm not that soft in the head."

"I see your point. Well, things must be really rough if colonels are deserting. This is interesting." Cal fingered the gun but the muzzle no longer pointed at Zen's stomach. "What are you looking for up here?"

"A place to hide out."

"For how long?"

"Hell, how long can this go on?" Zen answered. "Even when it's over, I don't want to go back down there and walk on skulls."

"Walk on skulls?"

"That's all that will be left."

"You think the Asians are gonna win, then?"

"I got a hunch there will be more skulls than anything else in Asia, too. No, I don't think they're going to win. I don't think anybody is going to win this one, except the people who have enough sense to hide."

Jake came out of his dreaming and put his hand on Cal's shoulder. "Kurt's all right," he said.

It was obvious that Cal did not think very highly of this recommendation.

"He's my pal," Jake continued. "Let him join us. He'll make a good hand. Besides, me and him were buddies. And there was a girl—" He stopped speaking and broke into dark musing as the memory of his wife came again into his mind.

"Were you with this woman?" Cal asked.

"He never was with this woman in his life!" Jake screamed. "She was mine, I tell you. Mine!"

"Shut up, crazy head."

"Tell him, Kurt. Tell him Marcia was mine."

"Sure, Jake," Zen soothed. "Everybody knew you and Marcia were that way. Cal and I were talking about another woman."

"Oh. That's different. But I don't want to hear either of you say that Marcia didn't belong to me."

The wolf-faced man looked as if he was about to use his gun on Jake. "You stinking nut head, you stay out of this!"

"All I was trying to do was to tell you Kurt was my pal."

"All right, you've told me. Now shut up." Cal turned to Zen again. "About this woman, colonel? Were you together?"

"No," Zen said.

"But she yelled out to you when me and Ed grabbed her."

"I heard her."

"You did?" Cal's finger went around the trigger of the gun.

"Yeah. I was following her but I didn't know she knew it until she yelled."

"Oh." Cal kept his finger on the trigger. "Why were you following her?"

"Hell, don't be stupid!" Zen exploded. "Why would any man follow a woman like that?"

A trace of a grin went across the wolf face at this answer. Cal licked his lips. This was an answer he understood. "I don't blame you for that. But why was she coming up here?"

"That I don't know," Zen said. "I don't think it made much difference anyhow. As soon as night came—" He squinted at the sun.

"Do you think she might be a spy for Cuso heading for his camp to report?"

Zen felt his lower jaw sag. This was a thought that had not crossed his mind. He knew only too well that the Asiatic had spies in as many places as he could get them. Cuso's survival depended in a large degree on knowing how many troops were moving against him, how they were armed and over what passes they were coming.

"I see by your face that you had never thought of that," Cal said. "Then what is she doing up here?"

"I don't know. I realized she was ahead of me about a mile back. As to what she is doing, maybe she got tired of all that down there too, and decided to come up here and live in the mountains?"

"A woman in this wilderness?"

"Some women have delusions that they can return to the primitive and make a go of it."

"And maybe she had some other idea," Cal said.

Zen shrugged.

"Knowing this may be important to us," Cal said.

"Then we had better go ask her," Zen said. He was still shocked at the thought that Nedra might be a spy. Up until now, he had thought he was shockproof.

"You want to ask her?" Cal said.

"Sure."

"Okay, you do the asking. I'll listen. And don't get any funny ideas." His finger curled around the trigger of the gun. "Remember, that if a patrol should come looking for a deserter, they would only be going to shoot him. I would be doing them a favor if I shot him in advance."

"I covered my tracks," Zen said. "Nobody will be looking for me."

"How did you do it?"

"I traded dog tags with a hunk of meat that had once been a GI. There wasn't enough left of him to tell for sure what he was. The burial detail will clip my tags from his body and another colonel will be listed as killed in action. The GI will be listed as missing."

"That was smart," Cal said, approvingly. For the first time, Zen thought he detected a note of admiration in the voice tones of the ragged man.

Nedra was leaning against what had once been a work-bench in the garage. Her helmet was off, her hair was ruffled, and her tunic had been almost torn from her body. A look of pure gratitude appeared on her face when Zen stepped through the doorway. A little cry of gladness on her lips, she started toward him. Her eyes said she had never been as happy to see anybody in her life as she was to see this tall, lean colonel.

With her was the little bow-legged man. He didn't look happy as Zen entered. "Stand still," he snarled at the girl. "Who the hell are you?"

At his words, Nedra let her body sag back against the bench.

"Ed, this is Kurt," Cal said. "He's joining us."

The look in Ed's eyes was pure venom. "He may join us but he won't last long. This woman is mine. I saw her first."

Zen wished fervently that he had the carbine back in his possession. Some vermin did not deserve to live. But Jake had that weapon. While he could probably take the carbine away from Jake, the gun in Cal's hands was very steady.

"She's not mine, you know," he said to Ed. "So far as I am concerned, you are welcome to her."

"Oh, that's different," Ed said, relieved.

If Zen's words relieved Ed, they had the opposite effect on Nedra. She opened her mouth to speak to him, then closed it in an apparent effort to bite off words that no lady should use.

Cal laughed. "Ed is mighty touchy about his women. But don't let that stop you. Ask her what she is doing up here?"

"None of your damned business, either of you," Nedra answered.

Zen shrugged and spread his hands in a gesture which said that he hoped Cal would see how it was. Cal nodded. "We'll find out later." His manner indicated there was no question in his mind that he would find out what he wanted to know. "Right now it's time for chow. Jake, get on the job."

Jake turned and walked across the street to another house. Cal bringing up the rear, the others followed Jake. Ed took hold of Nedra's arm and escorted her across the street. Seeing this, Kurt Zen again wished that he had a gun.

CHAPTER VI

The meal was beef stew, which Jake prepared in a big pot on an old wood-burning range. They all ate around the kitchen table.

"There are lots of wild cattle up here," Cal explained. "This used to be good range country, you know. The remnants of the old beef herds are still in existence, the ones that have learned how to dodge or whip the lions, that is."

Zen was busy watching Nedra and Ed. The little bantam was following every move she made and was keeping as close to her as possible. He insisted on sitting next to her at the table and he kept trying to touch her at every opportunity.

Zen kept silent. Inwardly, he was greatly perturbed. Night was already throwing shadows over the mountains. What would happen after darkness fell? Trying to keep such thoughts out of his mind, he found himself wondering if it would be possible for him to break the bantam's neck with his bare hands. He decided he could do this, and that he would like to do it, but that he would also like to stay alive afterward.

"Girls who go walking in the mountains have to take what happens to them," he said.

Nedra ignored him. Ed glowered at him. Cal chuckled but continued eating without speaking. Jake ate as if he did not know what he was doing or where he was. Occasionally he looked toward the northwest and shook his fist in that direction. Zen knew that deep in his sick mind Jake was dreaming of what he would do to the Asians. Remembering Marcia, Zen did not blame him.

Ed tried to urge the nurse toward the dilapidated sofa in the room but she eluded him and sat on an empty powder can, to the obvious disgust of the bantam. Two people could not sit on the same powder can. Jake rattled dishes in the kitchen, and fought imaginary Asians. Cal found a seat in the corner, a position from which he could watch everyone in the room. Off in the night an owl hooted.

Ed jumped at the sound, grabbed Nedra's hand, and tried to drag her toward a ladder that led to some kind of an attic. Cal rose to his feet and moved toward the door.

"Stop it!" Nedra said, to Ed.

"But, honey, you've got to get out of here," Ed urged. The bantam was at the edge of panic.

"Why?"

"Because that owl hoot was a signal. The guys who are coming will take you away from me," Ed explained.

"Fine," Nedra said, her face brightening. "There is justice in the world after all. The good Lord does look after the poor working girl." Her voice indicated that she had begun to doubt this.

"But you don't know who these guys are," Ed protested.

"I don't care who they are. Satan himself would be welcome to me right now." The words were addressed to Ed but she was looking at Kurt Zen as she spoke. Zen did not attempt to answer her implied accusation.

"Damn it, I ain't going to let them take you away from me!" Ed shouted. Again he reached for the nurse's hand, to drag her toward the ladder. She slugged him in the mouth.

In a fury, his fists clenched, the bantam started toward her. She dodged behind Zen.

"Lay off her, Ed," Cal ordered.

"But she belongs to me!" Ed shouted. "You know I saw her first. You said so yourself!" The little man was beside himself with frustration and fury.

"If the lieutenant decides he wants her, you'll probably be the first one dead," the ragged man commented. Then he shrugged. "However, it's your funeral, not mine. Only you probably won't get a funeral."

Again the owl hoot sounded, just outside the house this time. Cal opened the door. A lieutenant and four soldiers entered. Zen took one look at the dirty uniforms and the slant eyes in dirty yellow faces and knew that these were Cuso's men. Coming into the room, the lieutenant took command.

"Who is this?" he demanded, nodding curtly toward Zen. He had not as yet noticed Nedra, who was still behind Kurt.

"A colonel who has seen the light of reason and has come over to our side," the ragged man promptly answered.

"Good. Cuso will be very glad to talk to him." The grin on the lieutenant's face left no doubt as to the meaning that lay back of his words. Cuso's methods of extracting information from any person careless enough to fall into his hands were well known.

"It will be a privilege to talk to the great leader of the Asian forces," Zen said. He felt sweat begin to appear under both arms. As soon as the lieutenant had appeared, he had known that Cal was a spy supplying information to Cuso.

"I'm sure Cuso will find it so," the lieutenant said. The grin vanished from his face as he caught a glimpse of Nedra behind the colonel. The rifle in his hands came up. "Who is that?" he demanded.

"A nurse who has also joined us," Cal hastily explained.

"What's she doing behind him?"

"Ed was urging her to go upstairs with him and she hid behind this man," Cal explained. A tic had appeared in the right cheek of the ragged man.

"Oh," the lieutenant said. His grin reappeared. "Come out, plizz."

As Nedra stepped to Zen's side, the lieutenant's grin widened. He sucked in his breath. "Yess. Oh but yess. Cuso will want to talk to her. Of that I am very sure."

Ed, his face as black as tar, started to protest. He took another look at the rifle in the Asian's hand and quickly changed his mind. The chattering of his teeth was audible all over the room.

"Why do you make that noise?" the lieutenant said, looking at him.

"It—it's cold in here," Ed stuttered.

As the bantam spoke, Zen noticed that the temperature in the big room seemed to have dropped far more than seemed reasonable. Even the opening of the door, and the admission of the cool night air, was not enough to account for the sudden chill in the room.

This cold was different from anything Zen had ever experienced before. It seemed to start at the center of the bones and work its way outward, reaching the skin surface last of all, where it produced a prickling sensation.

"I wish to eat," the lieutenant said.

"Of course," Cal instantly agreed. "Jake! Food for the gentleman."

Jake, his eyes murky, was standing in the door leading to the kitchen. The expression on his face indicated that he was about to launch himself at the Asians.

"Get into that kitchen!" Cal shouted.

"Oh, all right," Jake answered, moving out of sight. The banging of the pots and pans that followed his departure seemed to have a sullen sound.

"That one is not right in the head," the Asian officer said.

"He's just dumb," Cal said, defensively.

The lieutenant pursed his lips. "I forgot to mention that I left some of my men outside."

"Bring them in," Cal said promptly. "They're probably hungry, too. And cold."

"I think I shall leave them where they are," the lieutenant said, decisively. "I left them on guard. They have set up a mounted machine gun at the edge of the street."

"I see," Cal said.

"The gun covers this house," the officer continued.

"Oh," Cal said. A sudden shiver passed through his body. He knew perfectly well what the lieutenant had just told him.

It seemed to Kurt Zen that the temperature of the room had dropped another ten degrees. He was shivering, too, from the effect of that strange cold that seemed to start at the marrow of the bones and spread itself outward.

Of all those in the room, Nedra was the only one who did not seem to be suffering from the effect of the chill. Her eyes were bright and her face had a warm glow. Zen watched her out of the corners of his eyes. Didn't she know that she had escaped from Ed only to fall into the tender mercies of Cuso's men?

"What has happened to you?" he whispered to her.

Turned toward him, her eyes had a glow that seemed to come from some light that was suddenly burning inside them. The glow went from purple to violet, then to ultra-violet. After that, Zen could no longer see the glow, but he suspected it had gone into higher ranges still. What was more surprising was the fact that she was no longer frightened. Confidence had suddenly come to her, seemingly out of nowhere.

"What do you think has happened to me?" Her voice had changed too. All tension had gone from it. The ragged edges of conflict had disappeared. She seemed to be mistress of the situation, and to know it.

Jake came from the kitchen. "I pick up vibrations," he announced, his voice shrill.

"Get into the kitchen," Cal ordered, as the lieutenant raised his gun.

"But I'm only trying to tell you something."

"I'm telling you something, get back into that kitchen!" Cal ordered.

Jake's gaze went murkily around the room but it was obvious that he was giving more attention to some internal sight or sound than to the people present.

"Git," Cal shouted.

Jake backed from the doorway.

The lieutenant lowered the muzzle of the gun. He barked an order to the men with him, who arranged themselves with their backs to the wall. The officer moved toward the fire, where he settled himself in a chair.

"You," he said. "Take off my boots!"

He was speaking to Zen. Kurt measured the distance to the lieutenant's jaw. Out of the corners of his eyes, he noted the positions of the Asian soldiers.

"Odds are too great," he thought. "Stay alive now. Maybe your turn will come."

As he started to kneel, he bumped into Nedra, who was already on the floor unbuckling the officer's boots.

"If you would rather do it, I would rather have you do it," the lieutenant said, smirking.

"It is a privilege, sir," the girl said. She pulled off the heavy boot and began to peel off the thick sock.

The probability that she had saved Kurt Zen's life was very great. He felt a surge of anger at his own helplessness.

The feeling of cold at the marrow of his bones was appearing again. It was stronger now. He noticed that Cal's hands were trembling. The teeth of one of the soldiers standing against the wall were chattering audibly. A second soldier looked as if he were about to go to sleep.

Zen discovered as he yawned that he was getting sleepy too. Along with the cold creeping outward from his bones was a sensation of mental fogginess that was very close to sleep. The lieutenant, sitting directly in front of him, was nodding.

Everybody was getting sleepy! Why? Had some subtle, odorless gas been introduced into the room? What gas? Who had introduced it?

Crash!

The rifle in the hands of the nodding soldier slid out of his grasp and struck the floor, exploding as it hit. The slug ripped a hole through the wall, passing within a foot of the lieutenant's head.

The Asian officer was instantly on his feet. He spun to face the sound.

The soldier who had dropped the rifle slid forward on the floor and lay there, snoring.

As he saw what had happened, the face of the lieutenant settled into a grim mask. He pressed the trigger of the automatic weapon he carried. The gun burped violently. The sleeping soldier jerked as the heavy slugs crashed into his body. A little trickle of blood ran from his nose and collected in a small pool on the floor. The man died where he lay.

"*Yen thotem ke vos!*" the lieutenant snarled. Two of the soldiers left their position against the wall and lifted the body of their dead comrade. The third remained motionless against the wall while they carried the dead man out.

"If you go to sleep on me!" the lieutenant said, to the third soldier. His meaning was clear. The soldier shook his head. He understood what his officer meant. Terror was in him. But something else was in him too.

Zen watched the soldier fight this something else. Slowly, he let the butt of his rifle slide to the floor. He had enough intelligence and enough strength left not to drop the weapon. He set it against the wall. Then he sat down beside it.

He was making every possible effort to resist sleep, but in spite of everything he could do, he was losing this fight. Slowly, a fraction of an inch at a time, his head slid forward. Finally it dropped on his arms that were folded across his knees. He began snoring.

The face of the lieutenant was that of a frightened tiger from the depths of the Assam jungles. The muzzle of the gun swung to cover the sleeping soldier. A split second passed during which this Asian was on the verge of joining his ancestors.

Realizing finally that this man could not be held accountable for his inability to stay awake, the lieutenant held his fire. He jerked up his head to stare around the room. His face was that of a tiger who suspects it has been caught in a trap but is not yet certain of the nature of the device it has been snared in. His eyes came to focus on Cal.

"I—I swear—" The ragged man's voice was a thick mutter that did not convey much meaning. Cal was sleepy too!

"What have you done here?"

"I—nothing. I have done nothing—and I know nothing—I am as surprised as you."

"You're a liar!"

"No. Telling truth—" Cal's head had sagged downward toward his chest and his voice was getting thicker and more groggy. With an effort of will, he snapped his head up. "I—don't know. Something.... Yes! Never heard of anything like it before.... Hell, lieutenant, it's getting me too!"

Cal's head sagged forward on his chest. "So sleepy ... so tired ... gotta take a nap...." His knees sagging, Cal lay down on the floor. He cuddled his head on one arm.

The lieutenant spoke, but the grunt that came from his lips was not a growl. Soon, he, too, was fast asleep.

Kurt and Nedra were the only two people who were able to remain awake. The nurse was making desperate efforts to resist this strange sleepiness. Swaying on her feet, she turned toward Zen. He caught her in his arms.

"What's happening?" She sounded like a tired little girl.

"I don't know," Zen answered.

"Why is everybody going to sleep? Is it bedtime?"

"It must be."

"Are you sleepy, too?" Her voice was a tired whisper.

"I never was so sleepy before in my life," Kurt answered.

"Then why don't we—just take a little nap?" Nedra murmured. The way she spoke, this was the most reasonable suggestion that had ever been offered. Sagging into his arms, she would have fallen if he had not caught her. Gently, he eased her to the floor. Her chest rose and fell in a regular rhythm.

If there was one thing Kurt wanted to do it was to lie down on the floor and go to sleep, too. Every organ in his body, every cell, every molecule seemed to cry out that sleep was needed. He felt his knees begin to sag, his head to droop. It seemed to him that all strength was going out of his body, that his muscles could no longer hold him erect.

"Stay awake!" someone snarled at him. He was startled to realize it was his own voice that had spoken the words. He was even more startled by the fury in the tones.

His knees continued to sag. In spite of everything he could do to prevent it, his body continued on its way to the floor. The muscles in his long legs seemed to have turned into rubber. He went down to his knees but caught himself on his hands.

The impulse to continue the rest of the way to the floor was like a tidal wave. Every thought in his mind was on the desirability of sleep. How wonderful it would be to take a nap, to rest, to dream, to wake no more.

With a strength that was born of desperation, he fought this impulse. A battle began inside his body, a conflict that seemed to involve every brain cell and every nerve ending, and finally every muscle group. Pain came up as muscle fought muscle, as nerve cell fought nerve cell, as one part of the brain fought another part. He tried to force his body to rise to its feet again.

All he could do was grunt.

"Stand up!" he snarled at himself.

His body quivered and twisted but did not move. He repeated the command to himself. The effect was to increase the conflict. And the pain. He had never known such agony. It rolled through him like a series of tidal waves.

Click!

What happened took place so suddenly that it seemed to occur outside of time.

CHAPTER VII

Instantly, as the click sounded, he was outside his body, looking down at it. The pain was gone. The conflicting muscle pulls were gone. Or he was no longer aware of them. He understood that the latter was the true explanation.

"Stand up," he said, to his body.

His body obeyed this order. It rose from its hands and knees and stood upon its feet.

This fact did not surprise Kurt Zen. He had known it would happen. This was the way things were. The essence of him, the consciousness that was above the body, was never surprised.

"Stop trembling," he said, silently, to his body.

Instantly the tremors vanished. The body knew its master.

Kurt Zen also knew that he now had a choice. He could go back into that body. Or he could go—elsewhere. But he knew where he was needed most.

Click!

The way he went back into his body was like turning a switch. One instant, he was inside, looking through his eyes, hearing through his ears.

He moved quickly, snatching the gun from the lieutenant's grasp. Another instant and he had the weapons of the soldiers. He flung these into the corner. Then he grabbed Cal's gun from the floor where the ragged man had dropped it.

At this point, he saw that Nedra was sitting up and was watching him. The expression on her face was that of a sleepy small girl awakening in the morning. Only this small girl did not quite succeed in looking as if she had been asleep. Her eyes were too wide open and she looked much too alert.

"Hello," Zen said. "So you decided to call off the sham." The thought popped into his mind and the words out of his mouth before he could stop them.

"Did you know?" she gasped.

"Of course I did," Zen stoutly insisted. "When you went to sleep, I knew it was a trick designed to lure me by suggestion into the belief that I was sleepy, too."

"Then why did you let me do it?"

"I wanted to see how far you would go," he answered. "Come on. Let's get out of here."

"What about them? Are they shamming too?" She pointed to the bodies on the floor.

"They're up there, watching," he said, gesturing toward the ceiling. He laughed.

Owlishly, she stared at him. "I do believe you are out of your mind, colonel."

"It helps," he said. "Come on. Let's make tracks."

"That's a splendid idea, colonel. Except for one thing."

"What's that?"

She pointed to the sleeping lieutenant. "He said he had left some men with a machine gun."

"Damn! I had forgotten that. However, that is a problem that can be solved."

"How?"

"This way." He moved to the heavy machine gun mounted at the window so that its muzzle covered the street. He had his finger on the trigger and was searching the street when he realized that she was pulling at his arm and speaking to him. "What?" he said.

"No," she answered. Her voice was very firm.

"Are you out of your mind?" he demanded.

"We don't have to shoot them," she replied.

"Why not?"

"Because they are already taken care of."

"Eh? How do you know?"

"I know."

"Then you also know how these men here were put to sleep?" His voice had the sound of steel on stone.

She faced him without fear. "Yes."

"You did it?"

"No."

"Then who did?"

"Come and I will show you."

"Hunh!" Zen grunted. He made up his mind without hesitation. Starting toward the back door, he discovered that she was going out the front. "But that door is probably covered," he protested.

She opened it without answering his protest. Going through it, Zen thought the night outside was far colder than it had any right to be. Nedra moved without hesitation. Fifty yards away from the house a machine gun mounted on a tripod was set up in the street. Two men were lying on the ground beside it. In the quiet night, Zen could hear them snoring.

"All right," he said. "I have to admit you knew what you were talking about. But if you didn't do this, who did?"

"Just a minute and you will have an answer to your question," she replied.

A block beyond the machine gun, a tall figure lounged in the doorway of a ruined building.

"Hi, kids," he said.

At the first sound of the deep bass voice Zen knew that this was West. The craggy man nodded to him. West did not seem in the least surprised to see Zen.

"What the hell are you doing here?" Zen said.

"I had business here," West said, in a tone of voice that made Zen feel like an errant schoolboy being reproved by a kind, but firm, teacher.

"Did you make those people go to sleep?" Zen continued.

"Has somebody been sleeping?" West answered. "Hmm."

"Yes," Zen said.

"Did you run into some difficulty?" West asked Nedra. He ignored Zen.

"Sort of," the girl answered. "The fact is, I almost got raped. I was afraid I wasn't going to reach you."

"I was busy and didn't pick you up at first," the craggy man said. His voice was a rumble of sound in the darkness. He did not seem surprised when she mentioned what had almost happened. "The colonel followed you, eh?"

"Yes. I told you he would."

"How did you know I would follow you?" Zen demanded. With the lieutenant's gun in his hands, he felt very secure.

"Any woman would know that," Nedra answered. Her laugh tinkled in the darkness. Finding Zen's arm, she squeezed it. "He is one of the new people," she said, to West.

Zen wished he could have sunk into the ground. The craggy man did not seem surprised. "Hmm," he said again. "That is nice." Reserve seemed to have appeared in the bass tones.

"Let's get inside," Nedra suggested. "It's been a hard day and I'm so tired I feel as if I'm walking on my leg bones instead of my feet."

"Sorry," West said, without moving.

"What's wrong?" Nedra asked. Alarm suddenly appeared in her voice. "Don't you believe he is actually one of us? I told you he was."

"I did not say I disbelieved you. But what if you are mistaken?"

"I can't be mistaken. He followed me, didn't he? That proves I'm right."

"Men have been following women since Bhumi started turning," West replied. "What if you are wrong?"

"Oh," the nurse said, a falling inflection in her voice.

"In that case, who would shoot him?" West continued.

"Oh," the nurse said. Her voice fell lower still.

"You know the rules. We cannot have anyone except true mutants."

"Yes."

"In case someone brings in a person who is not a true mutant, it is the duty of the person who introduced the interloper to dispose of him."

"I know," Nedra said.

"In this case, it would be up to you to shoot the colonel," West continued. "Could you do it?"

"Well, I wouldn't want to—" The reluctance in her voice was very strong. "But I would do it."

"I hope I don't have to hold you to your promise," West said. "But in that case, come on, both of you. That is, if the colonel wishes."

"You can't kid me," Zen said. "Neither of you are capable of shooting anybody." He spoke fearlessly but he felt a trace of doubt. Not one of the new people had ever betrayed their group. This indicated something. "Lead on. I'm following."

Nedra found Zen's arm.

"Would you cry, after you had shot me?" Zen asked.

"Y—yes."

"But that wouldn't keep you from shooting me?"

"No."

"Well, that would be nice, anyhow, though I do not see what good it would do me."

"You sound as if you wouldn't care," the girl said.

"There are times when I am sure death would be a blessed relief." Zen meant every word he said. "That life down there," he jerked his thumb to indicate the lower ranges and the plains so far below, "gets tiresome. That's an understatement, if I ever made one."

The nurse was silent. "Yes, I understand," she said at last. "It was that way with me, once."

"How much farther before we get to—Hell, where are we going anyhow?" Zen blurted out.

"To the center here," Nedra answered.

"Um," Zen said. He wanted to say something else but he decided he'd better be careful.

West led them into an old tunnel which bored straight into the side of the mountain.

CHAPTER VIII

"Is the center in here?" Zen asked.

"Of course," Nedra answered.

"But why haven't Cal and his buddies found it?"

"They don't even know we exist," Nedra explained. "And if they did, for some reason they wouldn't like to come into the tunnels."

"In effect, the tunnel is wired," West said.

"Do you mean they would get a jolt of high voltage electricity if they ventured in here?"

"Nothing as crude as that," the craggy man replied. "However, at two places, high frequency generators are built into the walls and hidden in such a manner that a person entering the tunnel is saturated with their radiations, which trigger the adrenals in his body. The result of this is that he suddenly feels very much afraid."

"Eh?" Zen said, startled. "A fear generator?"

"In effect, it is that."

"But that would be a very powerful weapon."

"Yes, it would," the craggy man said, his voice dry.

"If you could generate such radiations in sufficient intensity and cover a large enough area with them, you could panic a division, perhaps even an army." Excitement was in Zen's voice. He knew that the scientists were desperately searching for a new weapon that might possibly end the war. Perhaps here was such a weapon.

"It might work that way," West admitted.

"Does the government know about this?"

"I believe not."

"Who invented it?"

"I believe Jal Jonner is generally credited with being the inventor," West said.

"Oh," Zen answered, and was silent. Jonner's name had become a legend of the days when there were giants in the Earth, mighty men whose thinking had gone beyond the concept of nations to envision one race, beyond the creeds of churches to see one faith, and beyond the dogma of economics to state that as long as one hungry man existed on the face of the earth, no man with a full dinner in front of him was free to eat his meal in peace and safety. Jonner's thinking had also gone beyond one planet to see one solar system—and beyond that, one universe.

"Here is the first generator," West said. He flicked the beam of his flashlight against the walls. "Of course, there isn't anything to see. But you may feel something."

As the intelligence agent moved forward, a sudden surge of fear came boiling up from his middle. It was a wild emotion and it carried with it a blasting sense of great peril, of death. Instantly, thoughts flashed through his mind of the first time he had ever been under shell fire, the scream of artillery shells, the blasts of the explosions, the shaking of the earth.

As the surge of fear shot upward from his middle, he felt his body jerk and start to tremble. "Run!" a voice screamed inside him. "Get away from here! Run for your life!"

He caught the impulse to flee, held it in check. It was like trying to hold back a tidal wave. "This is an interesting effect," he said. "Does the generator have the same effect on all people?"

West grunted and walked ahead without answering the question. Zen thought the grunt held an approving tone. Nedra squeezed his arm but said nothing.

The craggy man did not point out the second generator, but Zen felt the radiations hit him, stronger than before. He was mentally prepared this time, but his body wasn't. He felt his muscles tie themselves into knots. The impulse to run was a screaming ululation of mad wolf intensity pouring into his consciousness.

Zen kept on walking. As abruptly as he had entered it, he was out of the radiation zone. Up ahead of him, West did not grunt or change his pace. Except for Nedra's fingers digging into his arm, Zen had no indication that either felt the radiation. What kind of people were they, to be able to walk through hell and be uninfluenced by it? Zen wondered as he wiped sweat off his forehead.

Ahead, West grunted and played his light on the side wall. The craggy man grunted again. On the right, the side wall began to swing back as a door opened there. From the tunnel the wall looked like solid stone, but as the door opened, the back was seen to be made of metal. A lighted tunnel leading to a large gallery lay beyond.

"Enter," West said.

"Who did all of this?" Zen inquired.

"Jal Jonner took over the title to this old mine. He and his men sealed off the deeper tunnels, enlarged them, provided an air supply, built laboratories and living quarters, and made a comfortable hidden world here."

Zen felt he should have known better than to ask. According to these people, Jal Jonner had done everything, except lay the foundations of the world. "I see," the colonel said. "He did all of this before he died." None of the reports he had read had mentioned this activity, or had even hinted at it, but he did not see fit to mention this.

"No," West denied.

"But you just said—"

"He did it after he died," the craggy man explained.

"Huh?" Zen said. "Pardon me, but I did not seem to hear you clearly. I thought you said he did this after he died."

"That's what I said. That's what he did." The craggy man's voice was calm.

"I—uh—" Zen hastily changed his mind about the words he was going to use. Secretly he was wondering if West was hopelessly insane. How could a dead man build anything? "You understand that I am not too familiar with what actually happened. Sorry and all that but I simply haven't had to learn."

"I understand," West said. "You don't need to apologize. You will learn here."

"Good," Zen said. He doubted if he felt better because his explanation had been accepted. West's last words had an ominous ring to them.

"Your lack of familiarity with Jonner's history is very obvious," West continued.

"But if he was dead—"

"He didn't die," West patiently explained. "He was buried. A handsome monument was erected over his grave. But he wasn't in the grave."

"Son-of-a-gun!" Zen said. "Why all the fol-de-rol?"

"To deceive curious intelligence agents," West said, with no humor in his voice.

Zen ignored the ironic threat. He was inside, this was what mattered. Also the idea of one of the world's foremost scientists—and Jonner had been exactly that—hiding himself away here where he could work undisturbed with others who shared his dream, intrigued him. Or had that dream been a grim prognostication of the way things were to be on the surface of the third planet out from the sun? Had the work here been an effort to escape that future? Was this underground cavern really a modern Ark, dug into the heart of a mountain so that at least a few humans might escape the deluge by fire?

Had a modern Noah appeared and not been recognized?

The thought shocked Kurt Zen. Somewhere he had read a prediction that Earth would be destroyed by fire. Here was evidence that possibly at least one human being had taken that prediction seriously enough to build a bomb-and-radiation-proof shelter!

"You seem to be thinking seriously," West observed.

"Perhaps for the first time in my life, I am doing exactly that. My brain seems to be trying to spin."

"Ah? Are you surprised at what you find here?"

"No. That is, not much. Mostly, I'm pleased."

"Good." West seemed satisfied. "Here comes John to greet us."

The craggy man's face lit up as a tall youth emerged from an adjoining tunnel and came forward to meet them. His greeting to West had respect in it, he merely glanced at Zen, but it was the nurse who commanded and held his interest.

"Nedra! You're back!"

"Of course I'm back, John." As if this were the most natural thing to do, Nedra allowed herself to be taken in John's arms. West smiled benevolently at the two. Zen carefully looked in the other direction.

"This is Colonel Kurt Zen, John," West said, when the two had finished kissing.

The tall youth extended his hand and said he was glad to meet Kurt. His face was brown, his cheeks were lean and slightly hollow, but his eyes were clear and his grip was firm without being bone-crushing.

"I imagine Kurt is rather tired," West said. "If you would find quarters for him, John—"

"Glad to do it," the tall youth said. "Come with me, Kurt."

Zen nodded goodnight to Nedra and to West and followed John away. He was tired down to the bottom of his thick-soled boots. Fatigue lay in layers through his muscles and along his nerve trunks. He knew he was keeping himself from collapsing only by an effort of will.

"I'll give you my room," John said.

"I couldn't think of depriving you of your quarters, old fellow," Zen protested.

"It's no deprivation. Besides, I'll be with Nedra."

"Um," Zen said. The jealousy he felt almost made him forget how tired he was.

The room was as bare as the cell of a monk. The bed was a double decker with the top deck covered with books. It was hand-made, of rough pine posts, and the springs were cords. There was no mattress. And no pillow. A reading lamp was at the head.

"Hope you're comfortable here," the tall youth said. "Is there anything I can get for you?"

"Nothing. But you might show me the little boy's room."

"Are you still on that level?" The tall youth seemed genuinely surprised.

"Yes," Zen said. Then, as the implications back of the question caught him, "Aren't you on the same level? I mean, don't you go?"

"Well, yes," John answered. Embarrassment reddened his face. "But you're older than I am, and I thought perhaps you—" His voice trailed off into silence as his embarrassment grew.

"You thought what?" Zen continued.

"Well, that—" The youth became flustered, then seemed to become irritated with himself for being flustered, then for being irritated. Zen watched the emotional reaction build higher and higher. He could see no possible importance in the emotional response of the tall kid except that the kid had intimated that he might be spending the night with Nedra. Would people who didn't use toilets spend nights together? If they did, what would they do? Talk about the beauties of flowers and read poetry to each other? Zen sniffed silently to himself, to show his contempt for such antics.

"I'll show you where to go," John said, suddenly.

Zen followed the tall youth out of the room and into a short tunnel which led to a large gallery. Here the old-time miners had found a sizeable body of ore. The gallery had been cleared of refuse and a number of small rooms had been dug into the walls, the whole place being illumined by a fluorescent paint that covered the walls. The color of the light was a misty blue and the whole big gallery seemed to float in this light, creating an effect that was breath-takingly beautiful.

In the first room they passed a naked young woman who was going through gymnastic exercises in time to slow music. At the sight of her lithe, brown body bending and swaying in time to slow music, Zen whistled appreciatively through his teeth. She was almost enough to make him forget Nedra.

In another room a fat youth was reading a book. He was lying flat on the floor. In a third, a skinny young man with skin the color of old ivory was sitting cross-legged before a shrine. His features were as immobile as a statue of Buddha. The same faint smile seemed painted on his face.

In another room a beautiful young woman was undressing preparatory to retiring. She hadn't bothered to close the door.

"What the hell is this, a glorified whorehouse?" Zen blurted out.

"A *whore house*? What's that?" John asked.

His manner made Zen feel like apologizing for having used such words in his presence. "Never mind. I withdraw the question. Who keeps tab on where the boys and the girls spend the night?"

"No one," John answered, astonished. "Is somebody supposed to?" He was startled at the idea. "Oh, you are concerned about sex. You are also new here. Sex is no problem here, as you will learn."

"No problem? Don't you engage in it?"

"We have other, and more important things, to do," John answered. His words were lofty but his tone was kind.

Zen heard the words but he filed mental reservations about accepting their meaning. Silently he wondered if these kids had all their marbles. Apparently they had not even learned about the birds and the bees.

"Anything else I can tell you?" John asked.

"You've already told me too much," Zen answered. "I'm afraid to ask you any more questions."

The toilet had no flush plumbing. *After use, press the button*, a sign above it said. Zen did just that. No sound of running water followed but the colonel had the dim impression that intensely bright light had flared for a moment. He did not have the courage to look and see what had happened.

In some ways, this toilet which disposed of its contents in a flash of light was more significant and possibly more productive of concern than Cuso's blooper or Cuso's lieutenant had been. If the new people found it convenient to disintegrate their sewage, rather than dispose of it by the conventional method, what else could they do?

Zen shook his head to indicate to himself how amazed he was. John thought he wanted more information and started to ask a question, which the colonel hastily interrupted. "Don't tell me any more. There are limits to what my liver and lights will stand."

"What have your liver and lights to do with this?"

"Nothing at all. That was only a figure of speech."

As they returned through the gallery, he saw that the bronze girl was still going through her rhythmic dance in time to the slow music. The sight of that perfectly formed nude body slowly swaying in the small room sent such a surge of excitement through Kurt Zen that he hastily turned his eyes away. If he was going to live in this place very long, they would have to make some new rules. How could any human being stay in bed alone when that beautiful bronze creature was going through her swaying dance?

"What is she doing, learning to be a strip-tease dancer?" he asked.

"Perfect muscular control. This is one of the exercises we all learn," John answered. "What's a strip-tease dancer?"

"Nothing you ever heard of," Zen answered. "But while she is developing her muscular control, what is she doing to the endocrinal system of every male in the place?"

"Not a thing," John said, astonished again.

Zen had grave doubts that the tall youth knew what he was talking about.

John selected a single book from the top of the double-decker bed, and anxiously inquired if there was anything more he could do to make the colonel comfortable for the night. Upon being told there was not, he departed with the book. Zen thought of the book benignly. If the tall youth was going to spend the night with Nedra, at least there would be a book between them.

He slid off his heavy pack and set the lieutenant's sub-machine gun where he could reach it readily. His counter told him there was no radio-activity present.

Books were in a niche in the stone wall behind the bed. The author of one caught his eye: Jal Jonner.

The name was enough to hold his attention. Jonner was known to have written books, but few had survived. Even the Library of Congress did not have them, but there was no Library of Congress in any sense of the word any more. When Washington had left the planet, the Library had gone with it.

Glancing at the introduction, Zen forgot all about his fatigue and where he was. One glance at the words and he knew he was in contact with the living waters of life itself.

INTRODUCTION

In the beginning, I am going to make an inaccurate statement. I am going to say that the reading of this book may open a new life for you. Now let me explain why this statement is inaccurate.

In the first place, it is inaccurate because this is not the start of your life. That took place millions of years ago—more millions of years than I care to mention here.

So your life did not start with the reading of these words.—Now as to the use of the word "new." This, also is inaccurate. To you, the ideas expressed here may seem novel and new. But they are not new in the sense that they have just been created, or even that I have cre-ated them. They were implicit in the formation of the first molecule of protoplasm that came into existence on this planet. They are, therefore, as old as life.

The pattern which you may, or may not follow, was laid down in the first molecule of protoplasm which appeared on this planet, as the Law of Growth.

However, there is no law which requires that one species on this planet, or even all combined species, the total life spectrum here, shall survive to grow to full stature. The possibility of growth is implicit in every form of life; it is latent, and capable of development, in every species. However, the species that fails to take advantage of the opportunity thus offered, if it fails to develop its potential, must inevitably give earth room to the species which is developing. In their day, the dinosaurs ruled the planet. They had their chance, but they failed to develop.

Where, now, are the dinosaurs?

The Law is—Grow or Die. THIS LAW ALSO APPLIES TO MAN.

This book may be regarded as a primer, a starting point of your adventure into the coming development of man. It is the first text book that you will receive. It is the beginning of the way.

How much progress you make upon the way, how well you master the law of growth, is, in large measure, up to you. You will receive assistance, sometimes without your knowledge, but it will not be the kind of assistance that will retard or weaken your development. The new people will not be helped—too much! Strength is required of them and strength is only achieved by overcoming obstacles.

The next upward step that the race takes—if it survives its own self-destructive impulses—will be of such a nature as to require the utmost in strength and courage from those who participate in it.

This step, it is fair to state, is in the direction of a higher development of consciousness.

Good luck—and God go with you.

Jal Jonner
The Big Sur
July 1971

Written in 1971, the book was now 49 years old, Zen decided after a rapid calculation. The war had started in 2009. The time was now 2020.

Eagerly, he turned to the first chapter. It seemed to him that his life was just beginning, that everything that had ever happened to him and all that he had ever done was in preparation for this moment, when life would begin.

After reading two pages, he reached the conclusion that, if this was a primer, the text that was to follow must be difficult indeed. The book started with mathematics that was twice as difficult as calculus. Trying to concentrate, he found the symbols blurring before his eyes. Then, as fatigue finally overwhelmed him, the whole page blurred and was gone. He was asleep.

But he wasn't really asleep. The body slept. But he was not the body. He was the consciousness that animated the body. This never slept.

He awakened at the touch of a hand on his shoulder.

CHAPTER IX

Coming back to conscious awareness, Kurt Zen simultaneously realized that something which he had been experiencing, and which had been very important, faded out of his memory like a gray ghost sliding silently away into a pearl-colored mist.

Nedra was shaking him by the shoulder and was smiling down at him. "Wake up, sleepy head. You've been snoozing for eighteen hours. That ought to be enough even for a growing boy like you."

Her face was radiant and alive. She looked as if she had just stepped out of a cold shower and had rubbed her beautiful body with a rough towel to bring the blood close to the surface of the skin.

"You look wonderful," Zen muttered, remembering what John had hinted. "Did you have a good night's sleep?"

"A couple of hours."

"No more than that?"

"I needed no more."

"Mm?" Zen said. He started to add another word, "Alone?" but managed to catch the question before it was out of his mouth. He examined her thoughtfully. "You look very contented," he said, without adding that in his experience women who looked so contented had only one reason for it.

"Why shouldn't I look contented? After spending so much time in the wilderness, I'm back on the stairway to heaven."

"What's the wilderness?"

"The world down below." She swept her hand in a gesture that included the unseen ranges and the plains below.

"Ah, yes," he yawned himself to wakefulness. "I was reading the most fascinating book before I dropped off to sleep. Here. I'll show you."

The book was not on his blanket. It was not in the wall niche. Nor was it behind the bed. "Hey, it's gone," he said. His eyes went around the room. He discovered other things that were missing. "The lieutenant's gun! And my pack!"

"Perhaps you just dreamed you had been reading a book."

"I didn't dream the gun and the pack. I carried both of them in here."

"I can explain about them. They were taken."

"Hunh? Why?"

"Weapons are not permitted here. Your gun and your pack were both taken for this reason."

"Hunh?" A growl came unbidden into his voice. He put these items out of his mind with the resolve to speak to someone about them at a later time. Something more important had happened. What was it? A memory of his dream flicked through his mind but was gone before he could grasp it. A frown on his face, he said, "I know—" As he tried to speak, what he had intended to say slid out of his mind.

"You know what?" Nedra asked.

"Everything."

Her face showed surprise. "This is a great deal for one man to know. Are you sure?"

"Yes."

"Positive?"

"Hell, yes!"

An emotion that was like a curtain opening and closing slipped across her face. "Well, in that case, tell me things."

"I would, except I can't remember 'em."

Doubt came into the violet eyes. "What you need is some breakfast. Your blood sugar levels are too low. Breakfast will take care of that." Her voice was firm and sure.

"That's one thing I need," Zen said, his voice equally firm. "But there is one thing I don't need—an examination by a head shrinker."

"A what?"

"A psycho," he explained. "I call 'em head shrinkers because that is what they do. Oh, maybe I need such an examination but I have no intention of submitting to it."

Breakfast consisted of cornmeal mush, fried to a golden brown, and served with butter and honey. There was no coffee but he had long since learned to do without it. He ate ravenously. "I'm hungry right down to the marrow of my bones," he said. "Where does all this grub come from?"

"We get it," Nedra answered evasively.

"What do you do, raid the low country for supplies, like Cuso's men?"

"No, colonel, hardly that. We are not thieves." Her face showed displeasure.

"Well, where do you get it? I don't know how many of you are here, but if you have as many as a hundred, keeping this place supplied calls for some doing." He was fishing for information on the number of people hidden in this old mine.

"Actually, very little food is needed."

"How come, don't they eat?"

"Are you reading my mind?" the girl demanded. "If so, you might as well learn right now that this is not considered good manners here!" Momentarily, she was angry. "And besides, if you do it again, I'll close off my thoughts to you."

Zen, with a forkful of mush halfway to his mouth, was so surprised that he tried to speak and to swallow the mush at the same time, with the result that he choked. The inference back of her words opened up wide horizons of speculative thought. Was mind reading actually commonplace here?

"I'm sorry you choked," Nedra said. She pounded him on the back.

"Why don't you put me over your shoulder and burp me?" Zen complained. "Lay off with that pounding."

"Do you feel you really need burping?"

"Aw, shut up," Zen answered. If she thought he had read her mind, did this mean that she was actually capable of reading his thoughts? Could all of these people read his mind? Had the nude bronze girl going through the rhythmic exercises known what he was thinking about her. Zen felt himself coloring. It was one thing to have the normal libidinous impulses of the male but it was quite another thing to have every woman know what he was thinking about her.

"Colonel, I do believe you are blushing," Nedra said, a twinkle in her eyes.

"I am not," Zen said. "Actually I was wondering—"

"Whether or not I could read your mind? I told you it was not good manners here."

"Good manners or not, you seemed to know what I was thinking."

"It isn't necessary to read your mind to know what you are thinking if a pretty woman is concerned," Nedra said, primly. "Your thoughts are written on your face."

"Uh!" For a moment, his confusion grew. Her understanding was much too acute. Was she playing games, making fun? If so, this was a game that two could play. "In that case, since you already know about me—how about it?" he said, looking boldly at her.

She understood his meaning. For a moment, the violet eyes showed sadness. They seemed to indicate that she was disappointed in him, that she had hoped for much better from him. Then a sparkle came into them. "I told you once before—"

"Yeah, I know. You are going to wash out my mind with soap. But let's not do it right now. I'm still hungry."

"You are one of the most perplexing men I have ever met," Nedra said, as she rose to fill his plate again. "Also one of the fastest—"

"I thought we were going to stay away from that subject," he protested.

"I intended to say fastest on his mental feet," she answered. "And if you don't stop interrupting me to make a play on words, I'm going to give you a hit on the head. After that, Sam wants to see you."

"Sam, huh?" he said, with no real enthusiasm in his voice. Somehow this morning, he did not relish seeing the craggy man. But there was the matter of the missing pack and gun to be taken up with someone in authority. He suspected that West was that person.

The craggy man was alone in the room to which Nedra took him when he had finished breakfast. West was standing with his back to them as they entered, staring out of a picture window that was set flush with the wall of the building. Turning, he nodded to them, then motioned to them to come and stand beside him. Kurt Zen looked out on one of the most breath-takingly beautiful scenes he had ever seen. Directly below them the cliff dropped away for hundreds of feet, a blank wall of sheer rock. To the left, climbing up into the sky, was the peak of the mountain, solid granite. They were just at the edge of timberline here. Lower, the trees began: spruce, fir, and aspen, marching downward tier on tier over a series of rolling hills that concealed more than they revealed. In the distance was the front range, a towering sweep of mountains that looked small but which Zen knew to be rugged country. He had climbed them too recently to have any doubts as to how high they were. And how rugged.

In the far distance cumulus clouds were visible, thunder-storms beyond the mountains.

"*Thy purple mountain's majesty above the fruited plain....*"

The words of the song came unbidden into Kurt's mind. Down below him was—America. Or what was left of it. A pang came up in his throat at the thought and he felt muscles pull and knot in his stomach. He had loved this land.

America had stood for freedom. Her sons had fought for it, on battlefields in every corner of the earth, from sun-baked equatorial Africa to the freezing bitter steppes of Central Asia. While her sons had found graves, fighting for freedom, something had happened to the freedom for which they fought.

Nobody knew quite what had happened, but it had gone away. Possibly it had been lost as emergency followed emergency on the international scene, possibly it had been strangled in red tape as regulation followed regulation on the national scene. The time had come in America, too, as it had come to foreign lands, when all actions that were not compulsory were forbidden.

Thus freedom had died.

"Do you feel as bad as all that, colonel?" West said softly. The man's face was grave and each ridge on it seemed carved out of another and harder kind of granite.

"It seems such a shame," Zen said. "I loved this land. It was my country. And I don't feel that I have to apologize for a gulp in my tongue as I talk about it."

"It is not necessary to apologize for loving one's own land, colonel," West said, his voice softer still. "You are not alone."

"Not alone?" Zen said. "From you, this talk sounds strange."

"We have all loved this land, too, colonel, and the principles for which it stood. That is why we are here." West's voice became softer still, but the gravity in his face seemed to increase.

"That is good talk," Zen said. "However, if I have learned one thing, it is that talk is cheap. You are outlaws hiding here yet you talk of loving the land that you have failed to serve." He felt his voice grate as he spoke.

"Bravely spoken, colonel," West applauded. A glint that might have been appreciation and might have been the edge of hidden anger showed in his eyes. "Particularly so since you are in the power of these—ah—outlaws."

"Very brave," Nedra agreed. "And very foolish."

"You did not bring me here to tell me that I am in your power," Zen answered. "Nor to comment on my bravery. Nor my foolishness."

"I think he can read minds," Nedra said.

"I do not in the least doubt it," West answered. "If he did not possess this ability, or almost possess it, he would not be here."

"I, in my turn, think both of you are nuts," Zen answered. "I'm not putting on a mind-reading act."

"Not consciously, colonel, of course," West agreed. "You think your thoughts are your own. Often they are. But there are also times when they have originated with somebody else. However, before you tell me that I did not call you up here to discuss your mind-reading ability, or lack of it, I will show you one reason why I wanted you. Take the glasses, observe the ridge in the far distance, just under the pines. Tell me what you see there."

"Horses," Zen said. "No, mules. With riders. Cuso's men going out on a raiding party looking for food, ammo, and women, if they can catch 'em."

"Quite right, colonel. Except that they probably have the additional duty of inspecting the damage their blooper did when it exploded."

"I hope they inspect that damage from close range," Zen said fervidly. "That area is hot. If they will only spend an hour or so—" He broke off as he remembered that both Nedra and West had spent too much time in the same hot zone.

"They will not be that foolish," West said.

"I know some people who were," Zen said.

"Perhaps the area, at least on the fringes, was not as hot as you had thought," West suggested.

"My counter said it was," Zen answered.

"Possibly your counter was in error. Now if you will come into this room, colonel." West moved through an archway in the stone wall and into another room, holding the heavy draperies aside so Zen and Nedra could enter. An opaque screen was set into the wall. Several chairs, including one large seat with control buttons built into the arms, were in this room. West closed the curtain over the arch through which they had entered and motioned Zen to a chair. The craggy man slid into the chair with the buttons on the arms. Nedra sat beside Zen. Relaxed and at ease in the chair, she seemed to have forgotten that such creatures as colonels of intelligence existed. West pushed a button. Light flicked across the screen, danced an erratic pattern there, and vanished. An image began to form. Firming, it increased in detail, and became a city.

Or what had once been a city.

The place was blackened now, the buildings lying in ruins. Towers had toppled, windows had broken, the ravages of fire were visible. Here and there tall buildings had crumbled into streets that crossed and criss-crossed each other at crazy angles. The rubble from the broken buildings still lay where it had fallen.

"Washington, by thunder!" Zen said. "This was their prime target. We stopped their bombers cold but they eventually got through with a guided missile. The city is still hot. You can see it right there on the screen. Not a sign of life!" He became excited as he re-lived those first mad moments when the Asian Federation had struck out of nowhere. In this moment what little freedom that had remained in America had been given up in the face of the seemingly more important necessity of remaining alive.

"Yes," West said. "Now what do you see?"

The ruined Washington faded from the scene. As it faded, the broken dome of the capitol building—its top had been blown off in the blast— was revealed looking like a mysterious crater on the moon open to the sea of space.

Another city came on the screen, a mass of broken buildings where two rivers met.

"I think that's Pittsburgh," Zen said. "They were eager to hit us there, to cut down on our industrial production potential. They got Gary, Indiana, and South Chicago, for the same reason. In spite of everything we could do to stop it, they eventually got through to our major production centers. If we hadn't foreseen the possibility of this happening, and had not spread our industry across the country, breaking it up into small parts, they would have crippled us so badly before the war even started that we would not have lasted long. However, even with our production spread, when they hit the sources of our raw materials, they hurt us—bad. Our stock piles gave out after a couple of years. Since then we've been scavenging for metal wherever we can find it."

"Yes. I know," West said.

"Of course, while they were hurting us, we weren't exactly helping them," Zen said. "We had a few guided missiles ready in their launching racks ourselves. We weren't exactly defenseless." Pride came into his voice as he spoke.

"I agree with you there," West said. "Would you like to see some of our results."

"Hell, yes," Zen blurted out, surprised. "Our photo ships have never gotten really good pics. Have to fly too high for that. Oh, we have turned loose a flood of pics that purported to show how we had bombed hell out of the enemy, but these were all re-touched, to boost public morale. But—how does this radar work? Do you mean to tell me you can actually see what is going on inside the country of the enemy?" Puzzled wonder crept into his voice. Behind the feeling was a keen interest. If he could use this radar to see into the country of the enemy, it was a very important invention, though West did not seem to realize this.

In war, information was always as important as weapons, and sometimes more so. Knowledge of the enemy's troop dispositions, of his strength and his weaknesses, was often more than half the battle.

West did not answer. Another city swam into position on the screen. Zen caught a glimpse of a single minaret standing among the bare ruins and hazarded a guess as to the identity of the city.

"Moscow?"

"Yes."

"Good. One of our fast planes sneaked over in full daylight, dumping his load. When the photo plane passed over hours later, the city was still burning. We really blasted the hell out of that dump!"

"You sound pleased, colonel. Do you know how many millions of people died directly or indirectly in that bomb explosion?"

"How many millions died in Washington, Pittsburgh, and Chicago?" Zen flared.

"Granted," West answered. "But after the first man has been killed, does it help the situation to kill a second? Or does killing the second one merely make it more likely that a third one will have to be destroyed?"

"What the hell difference does it make? This is war."

"That is also granted. However, the rules of life do not change because men declare war."

"Don't be so damned academic that you forget to be realistic. They were striking at our heart," Zen said, bitterness deep in his voice. "Look, we didn't seek this war. We did everything we could to prevent it. We tried compromise, arbitration, placation, and everything else we could think of. Nothing worked. They struck in the dark, without warning." As he spoke, his bitterness turned into deep anger.

"That is also granted," West said, while the ruined city was displayed on the screen. "But does it make a great deal of difference?"

Zen stared at the man, wondering what kind of a human he was. In the dim room, it was difficult to make out West's features. "It makes all the difference in the world. We believed in fairness. They ignored it. We believed in a better world. They would plunge us back into the night of barbarism. We believed in freedom. They wanted slaves. They set up a slave state and threw armed slaves against free men. We had no choice except to fight back."

"I see nothing to argue in all you have said," West answered. "Nor is it to my purpose to attempt to justify the actions of the western democracies. They need no justification. Nor do the actions of the Asian Federation need justification. In their eyes, they were right." His voice was a low monotone of sound without the trace of an emotion in it.

"Then what is your purpose?" Zen demanded.

"First, to point out that the human race is one organism. Viewed in its totality, it is just that, an organism. All the billions of individuals who compose it are cells in that organism."

"I am familiar with that theory," Zen answered. "A few crackpots have always insisted that we are a biological entity. But they have not succeeded in proving this."

"Haven't they?" West said. The slightest touch of irony appeared in his voice.

"Not so far as I know."

"Is it possible, colonel, that you do not know everything?" West asked.

"It is not only possible, it is obvious," Zen answered, unruffled by the cutting question. "If I knew everything, I wouldn't be sitting here talking to you. I would be out there winning a war."

"The point I want to make, colonel, is that the human race is divided against itself. Historically, this has been going on since remote ages. War after war after war."

"I do not see how America is responsible for the errors of history," Zen said. "We tried to avoid them. God knows we tried." Emphasis crept into his voice.

"I did not say these were errors, colonel," West replied. "I merely said they were history."

"But what point are you making if not the one that wars are mistakes?" Zen asked, surprised at the way the other's thinking had gone.

"I am making the point that war seems to be the way the entity, the human race as a whole, evolves. The method of evolution revealed by history is the pitting of one part of the entity against another part, then letting them fight it out to see which is the more efficient." A touch of grimness sounded in the voice of the craggy man. In the dimly lighted room, his face was as bleak—and as lonely—as the granite outcropping at the top of a mountain.

"This is a very savage philosophy," Kurt Zen commented.

"If I may disagree with you again, colonel, I do not think that this philosophy is necessarily savage. True, a great many men die in fiendishly ingenious ways. A great many women and children suffer. True, this system produces hunger in the world, and a fear so deep and so intense that the heart is hurt even to contemplate it."

"How can this be anything but savage?" Zen protested. "I don't care whether our side or the other side is doing it—it's still total savagery, utter barbarism!"

"But that is a short-term view and one which does not take into consideration all the factors in the equation. What is the purpose back of this savagery, if it is not to force men to learn and to grow? What if this so-called savagery is also the result of ignorance, of an entity trying desperately to learn how to solve a problem, but never quite succeeding?"

"But surely there must be some way which does not involve so much suffering," Zen protested. He was growing more and more uncomfortable. It was his impression that he was shifting sides in the argument without quite realizing he was doing it. Or perhaps West was the one who was shifting sides. This side-changing was producing confusion in his thinking.

"I have harbored the same hope," West answered. "However, I know of no way to accomplish this result. In a human being, we have a growing, evolving organism that is possessed of a keen brain and a vast curiosity. Such an organism, by its very nature, will have to try every possible road." West pressed a button.

Again the screen came to life. Dim and shadowy, human figures began to move there. Kurt Zen leaned forward to see them more clearly.

CHAPTER X

At first, the figures were indistinct and Zen could not see them clearly. He mentioned this to West.

"They will get sharper in a minute," the craggy man answered. His voice had sunk to a whisper heard from afar. Zen glanced at him to make certain he was still there. The colonel had the flickering impression that the chair was vacant but before the impression could firm itself, West, faster than the eyes could follow, seemed to be back in the chair. "Note the screen now, Kurt," West said.

The figures had become clear. It seemed to be a view of some kind of underground cavern where men were working on an object that looked like—Zen squinted his eyes, to make certain.

"A small space ship!" the colonel said. He felt eagerness rise in his voice. Like so many kids born in the age of science, he had harbored the dream of the days to come when men would fly beyond the sky, to storied space islands that lay afar. Science had promised that this would happen and the fiction writers had embellished this belief with dream worlds. Somehow, it had never come to pass. One problem after another had prevented realization of this dream. The war, which should have accelerated development, had stopped it completely. Neither side had the materials or the engineers or the skilled technicians to construct a vessel capable of space flight.

"No," West said. His voice was toneless and the far-away note was still strong in it. "Sorry to contradict you, colonel, but that is not a small space ship, though it is designed to get out of the atmosphere for a short time. Look again."

"Hell, it's a super bomb!" Zen gasped, as recognition came to him.

"Right, colonel!"

"A bomb big enough to devastate a continent!" Cold currents suddenly flurried at the base of Zen's spine.

"Right, colonel." West's voice was as dry as the Nevada wind.

"I didn't know we had such a bomb under construction," Zen blurted out.

"We haven't."

"Then who—where?" The cold currents at the base of Zen's back were flowing down both legs and up his spine.

"Look at the men, colonel. Look closely." West's voice was also cold.

"They're Asiatics!" Shouting the words, Zen was out of his chair. "I didn't see the yellow faces and the slanted eyes at first. West, that's a huge guided missile. It's being built to drop out of the sky at thousands of miles an hour, on us!"

"Yes," West said. He did not move a muscle in his body. On the other side of Kurt Zen, Nedra sat equally silent and motionless.

"I have to get out of here," Zen said. "This information must be reported to the general staff, at once!" Urgency pounded in the tones of his voice.

"The new people do not fight," West said. "I thought you were one of us."

"It doesn't matter who I am," Zen said quickly. "The building of this super bomb must be reported. *It must be!* Extra warnings must be issued. We must alert every z-type fighter we possess and have them in the air constantly, in the hope that we can destroy this bomb before it lands. We've got to follow the construction hourly, so we will know when it is ready to be launched. And that means we've got to have top-flight intelligence men here, to follow the building of that bomb every inch of the way. Or we've got to take this super-radar of yours to headquarters and use it there. That's the best solution, if it is at all practical." Zen was striding back and forth in the darkened room, planning the steps that had to be taken.

"West, do you realize this super-radar of yours will win the war!" Excitement tightened the colonel's voice. "With it, the enemy won't be able to make a move that we don't know about in advance." His excitement grew as the vast longing hidden in him for the end of the war tried to come to the surface.

"You have tears in your eyes, colonel," West said.

"You're out of your mind," Zen retorted. But he knew the craggy man was speaking the truth. He swallowed harder. "We've got the Asians cold. We'll know every move they make in advance." He exulted as he realized again how much this meant.

"I have always known every move they made in advance," West answered.

"We'll have them on their knees in—huh? What was that you just said? What was that?" Desperation appeared in the colonel's voice.

West repeated his words.

"Then why didn't you warn us?" Zen felt each word sting as it left his lips. "Why didn't you warn us? Why did you let so many of us die so unnecessarily?"

West did not answer.

The silence in the room grew deeper. Cold had begun to appear in the air. On the screen, the silent figures continued busily engaged in the building of their bomb.

"Don't you realize that your failure to report what you knew is high treason?" Zen continued.

The silence grew. West sat as solid and as immobile as a mountain. Nedra seemed to have shrunk in upon herself still farther. More than ever she looked like a very small girl who had somehow managed to intrude into a world of adults and was tremendously confused and hurt by what was happening here.

"Don't you hear me?" Zen said.

"I hear you," West answered. "Your loyalty to your country does you credit, colonel. It is to be expected from a person in your stage of development. However, you seem to have forgotten that I am not a citizen of your country. Or perhaps you did not know this?"

"Not a citizen?" Zen said. "But this mountain exists in America. I don't know whether it is actually on Canadian ground or lies in the United States, but this does not matter. By mutual treaty, the countries have become one nation. A citizen of one is automatically a citizen of the other."

"True, colonel." West did not attempt to explain.

"Then what country do you claim to belong to?" Zen felt his voice falter as he tried to grasp what lay back of this very strange man. "You talk like an American."

"I was born here."

"Then you are a citizen."

"No. I resigned my citizenship. As to my real country, it is a far land. I am sure you have no knowledge of it. My loyalty, colonel, is not to any nation on the face of the globe, but is to—growth, to the new people who will come into existence one day."

As West spoke, the cold that was freezing Zen's spine suddenly disappeared and was replaced by a sudden deep warmth. The words seemed to touch some hidden spring of warmth within him.

"My loyalty is to the future, to the growing tip of the life force, to what the human race will become, not to what it is today. Only the future has meaning, colonel, and to the building of that future I have dedicated my life."

In spite of the fact that the words thrilled him, Zen knew he had to deny them. "This is sophistry," he snapped. "I think any court in the land would hold it to be evasion of your proper duties. You can't continue living in a country and enjoying its ble—" Confusion came into Zen's mind.

"Were you going to say *blessings*, colonel?" West said, almost maliciously.

"Yes."

"Would you point out these blessings?"

"We had them once," Zen said. "And we're going to have them again."

"Are you?" West nodded toward the screen where the far-off enemy technicians and engineers were busy with their super bomb.

"Now that we know that it exists, that bomb will never land," Zen said. "I'll see to that personally."

"How are you going to discharge this responsibility?" West inquired.

"I'll find a way," Zen answered.

"I admire your spirit, colonel, though not necessarily your evaluation of your personal position at this moment. Also, there is one other thing that I want you to see."

The screen went blank. Slowly another scene formed on it. Zen, staring, blurted out words.

"That's another one. They're making two of those super bombs. I didn't think they had the materials and the technical know-how to make even one! This doubles the problem, and more than doubles the urgency. We'll have to guard the skyways from all directions, including straight up. Damn it, West!" Zen slapped his fist into his open palm to emphasize his feeling of urgency.

"Look again, colonel," the craggy man invited.

On second look Zen saw something that he had missed before. "Those are Americans! We're building that bomb!" His words were little gusts of explosive sound in the quiet room.

"Right," West said. His voice was very grim.

"Then it's a race to see which side gets its bomb built first?" Zen asked. He did not know whether or not he liked what his eyes were seeing and the interpretation his mind was giving him.

"I am afraid that is true," West reluctantly agreed. "But doesn't that change the picture, colonel?"

"How?" Zen demanded. "We're going to win a war. We've got to win it." The words were firmly spoken but somewhere a lingering doubt remained as if some point had not been considered.

"The other side also thinks it has to win," West pointed out.

"To hell with what they think. They started it. We didn't. Man, you don't intend to tell me that you are going to sit right here and watch two nations frantically try to destroy each other—and maybe the Earth with them—when you have the means to stop it in your hand?" Horror exploded in Zen's words.

"I am going to do just that," West stated. His voice was as firm and as solid as the granite core of a mountain.

"But you can't!" Zen expostulated.

"Why can't I?" West demanded. "I am not a citizen of either country and I owe nothing to any nation."

"Even if you are not a citizen of either country, you're still a human being. You owe loyalty to your own race," Zen said.

The craggy man showed faint signs of discomfort. But when he spoke, his voice was still imperturbable. "Granting your statement, what do you propose I do?"

"Stop the Asians," Zen answered promptly. "Give us complete information on the location of their super-bomb. We'll make certain we get ours finished first and we'll use it to blow their installation out of existence." At the moment, his plan seemed feasible.

"That would create the very danger you are trying to avoid, would it not?" West pointed out. "Both super bombs would explode simultaneously. Do you think the Earth would remain in its orbit if this happened?"

"I don't know," Zen answered. "That would be up to the astronomers and the astronomical physicists to decide. In any case, if the danger is too great, we'll use ordinary weapons to touch off their super bomb. Well get the job done before they finish."

"They are working underground, in a cavern at least three thousand feet deep," West pointed out. "Do you have a weapon that will penetrate to this depth?"

"We'll build one!"

"You talk very glibly, colonel."

"Somebody has got to talk!" Zen said fiercely. "Even if they are building their bomb underground, they must have an exit for it somewhere. We'll locate their exit and drop an H-bomb on it."

"And thus destroy their bomb and the best of their scientists and engineers?"

"This is war. You can't have sympathy in war."

"This is my point, colonel," West said patiently. "I have no sympathy—with either side."

"Then what do you propose—to sit here and do nothing?"

"I propose to let each side destroy the other as much as they wish and can. Then, when they have completely demonstrated the futility of their efforts, when it is utterly clear to the few who have survived that warfare is not the way to the future, then the new people will emerge to show the way to those who have survived." West's voice was calm. He seemed to be considering a situation often pondered and to be stating a conclusion firmly and definitely reached.

"But that involves senseless slaughter," Zen protested. "This was the reason that lay back of the dropping of the first atom bomb—to stop senseless slaughter."

"All slaughter is senseless, colonel, though from the viewpoint of the individual or nation doing it, slaughter is generally considered to be right at the time."

Zen started to comment on what the craggy man had just said, then changed his mind. Was he dealing with a madman? This seemed possible. West's words certainly did not fit any pattern that Zen knew. The act of sitting by and letting two nations commit suicide went beyond the bounds of rational thinking.

"I beg you, let me report this to the high command," Zen said, making one last plea.

"In reply, I want to ask one question," West answered. "What would happen to the people here, and to me, if I revealed the existence of this instrument?"

"You would be a hero," Zen said promptly, and knew he was lying as he spoke. "Your people would be protected."

"I dislike calling you a liar, colonel, but that is exactly what you are," West answered. "We would all be taken care of, as long as all of us did exactly what the high command wanted. The instant I tried to do anything else, my actions would be called treason and I would be considered a traitor. My equipment would be confiscated, '*for the convenience of the government*,' and I would be lucky if I did not face a firing squad. Tell me honestly, colonel, would not this happen?" For the first time, West's words had a tinge of anger in them. Or was it sorrow?

"Sam—" Nedra said. "Something—" Her voice was a whisper from some far-off land.

"What is it, Nedra?" West asked. In an instant, he had forgotten all about Kurt Zen.

The nurse sat up straight and stiff. All color fled from her face. "Something—" Her voice was the faintest whisper of sound in this quiet room.

"Nedra, what is it?" West's tones had alarm in them.

Instead of answering, the nurse slid from her chair to the floor, in a faint.

Dim and distant in the silence that followed came a popping sound.

Rat-tat-tat-tat-tat—

Zen had heard this death-dealing rattle too often to mistake its identity.

"A sub-machine gun!"

The drapes that covered the archway leading into this hidden room were shoved aside. A man fell through them. Zen knew at a glance that he was another of the kids who lived here in this hidden cavern inside a mountain. Blood was spewing from a hole in his back and he was fighting desperately for breath.

"They're—coming with guns!" he gasped.

West dropped to his knees and took the head of the youth in his lap. His face was dark as he saw the wound on the back. Cuddling the youth's head in his lap as one would a frightened child, he asked, "What happened, Carl?"

"I don't know. They came out of nowhere. There was no one. Then these men were here. They came—shooting." Blood came out of his mouth as he spoke. He tried to cough it away, and failed. His hand went to his mouth and wiped at the blood, then he lifted his hand to his eyes and saw what was there.

"How many are there?" Zen asked.

Carl's eyes wandered until he found the source of this question. "Dozens," he said, his voice dull. Blood was draining from his mouth across West's legs and was forming a pool on the floor.

Listening, Zen could distinguish three machine guns going now. Men were yelling. A girl was screaming. At the sounds, the colonel's lips formed into a line as sharp as the edge of a knife.

"How did they get past your fear generators?" he said to West.

"I don't know," the craggy man answered. "Perhaps they found an unguarded tunnel."

Zen could not see what difference it made how the intruders had secured entry. They were here. "Where are your weapons?" he demanded. In his mind was the thought that the new people would have weapons adequate to defend their own citadel.

"Weapons?" West did not seem to understand the term. "We have none."

"What?" Zen said. Hadn't West understood him. Every farmer, every rancher, and every householder had his stock of weapons. Almost all people went armed. "No rifles?"

"No."

"Not even tear gas?"

"No, colonel."

"Then how in the hell did you expect to stay alive?" Zen burst out. "You surely knew they would find you sometime."

"Staying alive is actually not as important as you think. Yes, son." West bent again to listen to the youth's words.

"Good—good—" The whisper was very faint.

West understood. "Goodbye," he said. "We will meet again. But, goodbye for now."

The youth sighed. All pain and all fear went from his face. Peace came to him.

But when West rose to his feet, his face was bleak. "He was new here," he said as if this explained something that he felt needed explaining.

Somewhere a woman was screaming. West listened to the sound, then started toward it. Zen caught his arm.

"The invaders have guns." His tone conveyed the impression that West was at fault because no weapons existed inside the mine. "Or do you want to go join him?" He nodded toward the body on the floor. Blood had stopped spilling from that body now. The essence of life had gone elsewhere and the tides of life had ceased flowing.

"Yes," West said bluntly. "I want to go with him." His face had grown more black. Heat lightning was dancing in his eyes.

Zen caught the impulse to say that this made two of them who wanted to join the bronze-skinned youth. He knew how to deal with this reaction.

"Okay," he said. "Good bye."

West blinked startled eyes at him.

"Run along," Zen said.

"Eh?"

"I'll take over here and fight the battle you are running from," Zen continued.

As if he were dispelling a mist from some hidden corner of his mind, the craggy man shook his head. "Sorry," he apologized. "However, the call is very strong. Only the sense of a job not yet done has kept me from going for—a long time." He shook his head again. "No, I shall not follow him, for another while, though I am positive that he is luckier than we are."

"I agree," Zen said.

Stooping, West picked up Nedra. She lay in his arms like a tired, sleeping child. Had she followed the youth? Kurt Zen had a moment of heartbreak as the thought passed through his mind before he saw that she was still breathing regularly.

"Follow me," West said.

The heat lightning still danced in the eyes of the craggy man as he moved across the room. The solid wall swung aside into another hidden door. "None of my people know this is here," he explained. "The combination lock is actuated only by my body."

As Kurt Zen went through the door he could hear the girl still screaming somewhere.

The passage was narrow. To one side, another passage led into a room where Zen caught a glimpse of some kind of electrical equipment in operation, the technical guts of the super-radar, he suspected.

Ahead, West growled, a sound that came from deep in his throat. He had stopped and was staring down into a hidden opening in the wall. Zen saw that the opening, through some hidden arrangement of mirrors, revealed the interior of the big gallery where he had spent the night.

Hell was loose in there now.

CHAPTER XI

Jake, Ed, and Cal were part of that hell. Each carried a smoking weapon in his hands. A body lay on the floor. Somewhere in one of the small rooms a woman was screaming. In the middle of the room stood the man who was obviously in charge of the situation. At the sight of this man, Kurt Zen felt his breath draw into his body so heavily that it whistled through his nostrils.

Cuso's lieutenant!

The others in the room were the Asians who had been with the lieutenant the night before.

"I should have slit their throats while they were asleep and in my power last night," Zen raged.

The only sound in the passage was that of West breathing heavily, like a man who had run a marathon and had lost. No, there were two men! Additional shock came up in Kurt Zen when he realized he was the second man. He seized the craggy man by the shoulder.

"West! They can't have that super radar. If we lose that, we have lost the war."

The craggy man did not move.

Anguish grew in Zen's voice. "If we lose this one, it will be the first war we have ever lost. And the last one. Nothing will remain to come after us except death and desolation."

"I know," West said. "The race soul will have to start over, in the swamps and on the mud flats, trying to rebuild the race with tools long since worn out and out of place in time." Again the tones of a bell were in his voice. But now the bell was tolling the death of a people, wailing that the glory that once had been was truly gone, wailing that the brave world that some men had tried to build was going into ashes and into doom.

"Do you believe in the race soul too?" West gasped.

"*Belief* is too weak a word. I *know* it exists."

Nedra sighed in West's arms and opened her eyes. Seeing who was holding her, she lay back in the arms of the craggy man, more than ever like a tired child. "What was it?" she whispered. "What's wrong? I—I took a little nap."

West set her on her feet and pointed at the opening. She clutched at the stone wall as she saw what was happening inside.

Running, the bronze girl who had danced to the slow music the night before, came fleeing from a room. One of Cuso's soldiers was pursuing her. She fled like a deer before some great hound that was interested in pulling her down but she did not flee fast enough. The soldier caught her and dragged her back into a room.

"West, how many of these kids did you have here?" Zen asked.

"About fifty," the craggy man answered. "I don't know how many are left nor can I guess how many will choose to stay alive if they are conquered before their training is completed."

"And no weapons?"

"None."

"What about my gun that was taken from me while I slept?"

"What good would one gun do now?"

"None, I guess," Zen said, helplessly. "But as they try to run me down, I'd like to have it in my hands. I'd at least take a few of them with me before they got me."

"We will survive," West said, his voice a mumble.

Zen pointed through the opening to the bodies lying on the floor below them. "They didn't," he said.

The craggy man groaned. "If I had time I would try to explain to you that survival does not lie in the body and can never be achieved there."

Zen answered, "I have no time for metaphysics. For purposes of defense, I'm taking command." He felt foolish as he spoke. What resources were his to command, what troops, what weapons? He knew the answer as the thought crossed his mind. If he only had the remnants of the broken column moving down the mountains after its disastrous encounter with Cuso's blooper. An idea came into his mind. Perhaps he could have these troops. "Where's my pack?" he demanded. His radio equipment was in that.

"It went with your gun into the deep hole," West said. "The deep hole is a fault the old miners uncovered here. It's miles deep." He shook his head.

"Damn!" Kurt Zen said. The depression in him was as deep as the fault in the mountain. "Isn't there any place where we can hide?"

"Many places," West said. "This whole mountain is a honeycomb of tunnels and shafts. We have explored fifteen separate levels and there are others which lie below the present water line." He did not protest at Zen's statement that the latter was taking command, but seemed willing to submit to the colonel's authority, and also interested in seeing how Zen would handle the problem.

"Then find us a place to hide until we can decide what to do to eliminate Cuso's men. A hiding hole first, then radio equipment. As soon as I can gain access to short-wave transmitting equipment, I can have a regiment of paratroopers on their way here."

"You sound as if you have authority," Nedra commented.

"I have."

"But you gave me the impression you were a deserter."

"They haven't discovered that yet, at headquarters. So far as they are concerned, I'm on a secret mission. And I haven't deserted the human race." Zen put sting into his words. The implication was that two people present were really deserters.

"Ah, well, colonel, we shall see about that." West had recovered most of his aplomb. Again he seemed to be observing from a great distance the antics of this strange species called human. But his face remained bleak and his eyes had flickers of lightning in them. He started away from the opening.

And stopped as metal clanged ahead of them.

A door opened there. An Asian soldier with his rifle at the ready came through. A second one followed the first. The rifles of both covered West.

Zen jerked his arms toward the roof. Neither the craggy man nor Nedra moved a muscle.

Slowly, West and Nedra raised their hands. At gun point, the two soldiers herded them toward the main gallery. At the sight of them the lieutenant hastily called Cal to him.

"Is this the one?" he demanded, pointing at West.

"That's him," Cal answered. "He's the leader here. He's the one you want."

Elation appeared as a shock-wave on the yellow face of the Asian lieutenant. Calling two men to him, he had West step aside, treating the craggy man with respect that bordered on deference but also with great firmness.

"You two stand against the wall with the others," he said to Nedra and Kurt Zen. There was no deference in his voice as he spoke to them. "If they move, shoot them!" he ordered his men. As Kurt and Nedra obeyed, the lieutenant drew West to one side and began a conversation with him. His men were still busy searching the old mine tunnels. Now and then they brought more captives to the main gallery.

Cal, Jake, and Ed remained in the center of the big room. Cal was trying to look important but the expression on his face indicated he was hiding guilt pangs somewhere inside. As soon as he saw Nedra, Ed's eyes became fixed on her though he did not look at her face. Jake's murky eyes were roving the chamber. He did not seem to comprehend what he was seeing but seemed to be living in some other world that was even more confusing and more clouded than this one.

The bronze girl, utterly naked, came limping into the gallery from one of the small rooms. She had a dazed expression on her face and she looked around the room as if she could not comprehend what was happening. At the sight of her, the lieutenant left off talking to West for a moment, his eyes glowing. But his conversation with West was more important than his lust. He motioned with his gun for the bronze girl to take her place against the wall. She stared at him as if she did not understand him. He waved the gun again.

Some dull comprehension of his meaning penetrated her mind. She stumbled to the wall but fell face downward on the stone floor.

Nedra, with a little cry of pity on her lips, moved quickly to the side of the bronze girl. Zen started to move, then stopped, but not because the rifle of one of the guards was swinging up to menace him. Nedra gave a quick examination of the girl, then got slowly to her feet.

"Dead?" Zen said.

"Y-es. But how did you know?"

"Just a hunch. What caused it, shock?"

"I imagine so. After she was violated, she wanted to die. So she really died because she wanted to. I—I—" Tears appeared in Nedra's violet eyes and ran down her cheeks. But she did not sob, though muscles moved in her throat.

West glanced at the bronze girl. He seemed to know, without being told, what had happened. His face became bleak. The lieutenant regarded the body of the dead girl with regret. When the soldier who had violated her came out of the room, the lieutenant ordered him to remove the body.

Zen got the impression that the lieutenant, even though he was talking earnestly with the craggy man, was waiting. Forty of the new people were herded into the room and forced to stand against the walls. Bronze striplings, they were. Not a one was out of his twenties and several were obviously in their teens. Though they were confused, they kept silent.

"Is this all?" Zen heard the lieutenant ask West.

The craggy man must have known at a glance the answer to this question but he took the time to count every person. "This is all," he said positively. The lieutenant seemed to believe him but Zen would have given odds that the man was lying.

The lieutenant continued to wait.

A guard, entering hastily, saluted. When Zen saw who was following the soldier he realized why the lieutenant had been waiting.

Cuso came into the gallery.

The Asian leader was a giant almost seven feet tall and big in proportion. He looked capable of killing a man with his bare hands, and probably was. Just looking at him, Zen knew why he had been selected to lead the airborne landing in America. Radiating power and strength, he was the type for this kind of mission.

Besides power, he radiated something else. Zen sensed this something else as a sickening feeling at the pit of his stomach, a tightening of muscles in the diaphragm.

When Cuso appeared, the lieutenant stiffened himself to attention and almost broke his arm saluting. He and Cuso spoke together in a sing-song dialect that Zen did not pretend to understand. As they talked, the lieutenant continued to point at West. A grin broke out on Cuso's face. He beckoned the craggy man to him.

The craggy man approached, but did not salute. Prisoners were not permitted to salute. Nor did he get down on his hands and knees, which was not only permitted but required among the Asians. West stood arrow-straight.

In spite of his disagreements with him, Zen felt proud of Sam West now. Cuso was grinning placatingly but in spite of the grin, West surely knew that he was looking at death, that the slightest show of resistance on his part would have only one result, although Cuso might save him until he had wrung all possible information out of him. Zen did not in the least doubt that information was what the Asian wanted first. After that, there was the tradition of torturing helpless prisoners.

"I have heard much about you," Cuso said. For an Asian, he spoke fair English.

"I am greatly honored," West answered. "However, I am curious as to how you heard about me."

A sly grin flitted across the Asian's face. "We 'ave our sources of information."

"Spies?" West asked.

"We 'ave spies, of course, but they could not find out much about you. There are other ways—how do you say it?"

"Clairvoyants?" West asked.

"Yes, that is right." Cuso looked pleased to be given the right word. He also looked startled because he had been given the right fact. Zen, listening, was surprised too. He knew that the suggestion to use clairvoyants to find out what the enemy was doing had often been made. As an intelligence officer, he had investigated several clairvoyants who had volunteered for this purpose. He knew that such a project had been set up but he did not know what the results had been, if any. However, to learn that the enemy had not only entertained the same ideas, but had used them with some success, startled him.

"I suspected clairvoyants," West said.

"Ah," Cuso said. "Did you also suspect that the only reason this airborne landing was made on these shores was to capture you?"

Even West's perfect control of his features could not hide the start of surprise at these words. "I am not that important," he said.

Cuso smiled deprecatingly and made a little gesture with his hand which said that such modesty was becoming in the truly great. Oddly, Zen had the impression that the Asian leader meant this. "As to that, I have the great privilege of offering you a commission as a field marshal in the armies of United Asia." His voice dripped oil and awe, oil because he was selling, awe because he was truly impressed by the rank of field marshal. Perhaps as a result of the successful achievement of this difficult mission, even he might have this rank. Hunger thickened on Cuso's face as he thought of this.

West blinked, then smiled back at Cuso. "That is interesting. But what makes you think I would be interested in such a commission—or in any commission—in your armies?"

"For protection, for one reason," Cuso answered promptly. "Our reports indicate that you are not a citizen of any country. Since this leaves you with no friends to protect you, this is an undesirable position. On the other hand, since you belong to no one, every country feels that you are an enemy. Because of this, your life is constantly in danger. However, holding our commission, you are automatically a citizen of United Asia, and thus are under our protection."

Cuso spoke as if being a citizen of United Asia was important and that holding a commission in its armies was even more so.

"Do you think I have no friends?" West asked.

"Well, you are not a citizen of—"

"Why do you think I need protection?" West continued.

The oily smile slid off of the giant Asian's face. For an instant, the wild beast underneath showed through. "Perhaps you do not need protection personally. But under the circumstances as I have outlined them, our mantle would automatically extend to the people working with you." His eyes went around the room to the youths standing rigidly against the wall. In this circuit, his gaze flicked contemptuously past the corpses lying on the floor.

The face of the craggy man got bleak again. He understood only too well what lay back of Cuso's words. "I see what you mean. But what do you wish of me?" His voice carried an intimation of surrender in the face of odds that he recognized as being hopeless.

Zen, with his back to the wall, tried to keep from squirming. Emotions that were causing actual pain were in his body. Why would the race mind permit such an outrage as this?

The smile on Cuso's face went from ear to ear. Here was victory, here was the submission of the enemy. Here was what his leaders wanted. Here was a marshal's baton for him.

"Really very little." He drew in his breath with a hiss as he addressed West, a sign of deferent politeness. "Merely that you show us what you have here. And, of course, that you should explain it all to our scientists and engineers, showing them how your equipment operates."

The room got very quiet after Cuso had finished speaking. West seemed to muse. "What do you think we have here?" he said.

"If I knew the answer to that question, I would not be asking such a stupid thing," Cuso answered.

"Quite true," West agreed. "I was stupid to even ask such a question."

"The time is here to end stupidity," Cuso said.

"Again I agree," the craggy man answered. He shrugged. "Well, when and where do you want me to start?" The smile on his face was a mixture of fear and resignation. It indicated that he had given up completely.

"Now you are talking the kind of words I like to hear," Cuso said emphatically. "You will start now, and show me, personally, everything that is of importance in this mountain."

"Very well. Follow me." West turned and moved toward the opening that led to the chamber where the super radar was hidden.

"Wait here," Cuso snapped at his lieutenant. "Shoot any person who moves."

"Yes, great one," the lieutenant answered, saluting. This was the kind of order he loved to obey.

Cuso and West went out of sight.

Jake, Cal, and Ed stood in the middle of the room. Ed approached the lieutenant, nodded toward Nedra, and spoke earnestly to the man. The lieutenant shook his head vigorously, a gesture which seemed to indicate that Ed was being very stupid. The bantam grumbled to himself and moved away. Out of the corners of his eyes he kept watching the nurse.

Nedra ignored him. She also ignored Kurt Zen. As silent as so many statues, the new people stood against the stone walls. They seemed stunned. The impossible had happened to them and they were having difficulty in adjusting to it. John was not in the room. Either he had succeeded in hiding or he had been killed.

The fat youth was standing directly across the gallery from Zen. Farther down the wall, clad in pants and a bra, was a shapely blonde. When he was not watching Nedra, Ed paid attention to her. His actions seemed to irritate the lieutenant. Lifting his rifle, he fired a single shot through the head of the bantam.

Ed collapsed, dead before he hit the floor. Two Asian soldiers carried the body away.

"That lieutenant is hell on lovers," Zen whispered.

Nedra did not answer him. Her face was pale and her breathing was shallow. A film of sweat glistened on her forehead. Glancing at her, Zen had the impression that she was listening.

For what? he wondered. The only thing that was left for any of them was the sounding of the trump of doom. Zen had no illusions that Cuso would keep his promises for any longer than was expedient. First, West and all the others must be pumped dry of information, the whole interior of the mountain must be thoroughly explored, then—more bodies for the deep hole.

Zen had no illusions that either West or the new people would long survive the information they could be forced to divulge. As to Cuso's talk of West being given a commission as a marshal of the Asian Federation, for protection, the colonel knew that Asian field marshals had been listed among the missing before now. A field marshal who fell from grace vanished.

Across the gallery the fat youth also vanished.

One second he was there, the next second he was—gone!

CHAPTER XII

Neither the lieutenant nor any of the Asians noticed that a man had vanished. Cal and Jake, with the memory of Ed's death still very fresh in their minds, were engaged in making themselves inconspicuous. As far as Zen could tell, none of these clean, tall kids knew anything out of the ordinary had happened.

Beside the colonel, Nedra seemed slightly more composed. Her eyes were blank as if she were not seeing. The thin film of moisture was still visible on her forehead. Zen started to whisper to her, to ask her if she had noticed anything different, then changed his mind. There was no point in taking such a risk at such a time.

A sound was in the room, a thin, high note that was close to the upper limits of hearing. It passed beyond the range of hearing, or diminished in volume, then came again with the frequency of the ears, moving like a microscopically small but very powerful honey bee. Had the sound been present all the time? Or had it come into existence just before the fat youth vanished? Zen did not know about the sound.

A face appeared in the middle of the room. About ten feet above the floor, it looked around briefly, then vanished.

Cal seemed to see it too. A startled expression appeared on the face of the ragged man. His eyes opened wide. He blinked them hastily when the face vanished, then looked furtively around the room.

Jake said, very loudly, to the face, "Hi, bud. Long time no see. Where you been?"

"Shut up your crazy head!" Cal snarled at him.

"But I just saw an old buddy," Jake tried to explain.

"You saw nothing."

"What are you two talking about?" the lieutenant demanded.

"Nothing," Cal answered. He pointed his finger at his forehead and made circling motions in the air, then nodded toward Jake. "You know he's a looney, lieutenant."

"Oh, yes," the Asian officer said, as if he had just remembered something. Again he lifted the rifle to his shoulder. Jake fell dead.

The lieutenant slid another cartridge into his rifle.

"As long as you needed us—" Cal began.

"But I no longer need you to help me find the hidden ones," the lieutenant answered. "That makes things different, doesn't it?"

"It sure does," Cal agreed. "But why did you shoot him?"

"I made up my mind months ago to shoot him as soon as I no longer needed him," the Asian officer answered. "He was too crazy to trust."

"But he found this place for you and he got you past those hell generators," Cal said.

"That is true. But the place is now found and we are past the odd devices that make weaklings afraid." His tone said that this also made the situation different and that the ragged man had better understand this and guide himself accordingly. Cal started to speak, then changed his mind.

"What were you two talking about?" the Asian asked.

"He said he saw a face in the air," the ragged man answered. "I told him that he was nuts and to shut up."

"Was there a face?"

"I didn't see nothing," Cal answered.

While the two were talking, Zen was watching a youth in a loin cloth across the room. Standing erect against the wall, looking as if he were being crucified there, but without making any sound, the youth was slowly vanishing.

While the youth was sliding away, the violin note throbbed softly in the air. As he vanished, it went into silence, ending on a note of triumph.

The lieutenant became suspicious. He scanned the people against the wall.

"I thought there were more—" he muttered. Slowly he counted them. "Thirty-eight," he said. As if to engrave the number on his memory, he repeated it.

Simultaneously, one of the Asian soldiers spoke to him in a swift flow of sound.

Zen could not understand what was being said, but he guessed from the way the soldier pointed to the spot where the fat youth had stood that he was reporting what he had seen happen.

While they were talking the face appeared again in the air high in the middle of the room. The face was that of a man. He was wearing a mustache and he looked around the room with alert brown eyes. Nodding to himself with apparent satisfaction, he vanished.

Down the wall from Zen, a young woman vanished.

She went rapidly, in the flicker of an eye.

A youth standing next in line to her, followed suit.

Turning, the lieutenant saw that something had happened. Hastily he counted those standing against the wall.

"Thirty-six! Who slipped out while my back was turned?"

As he asked the question, three of the new people vanished behind him. No one answered him. He turned again, and realized that more blank places had appeared while he was not looking.

Again, keeping behind him, another one of the new people vanished.

Watching, Zen was treated to the spectacle of seeing an Asian officer grow crazy. While the lieutenant was watching one particular person, nothing happened to the one under his scrutiny. But directly behind him a person flicked out of existence.

For a time, the lieutenant almost had Zen's sympathy. The colonel knew what would happen to this officer when Cuso returned and found his prey had been permitted to escape. The Asians were not known for leniency to their own men who failed an assigned duty.

The lieutenant knew as well as Zen what would happen to him. But he was helpless. No matter which way he looked, his back was always turned to someone. The person he was not watching—vanished.

Unnoticed by the lieutenant, the face that seemed to be directing the vanishing operation appeared and disappeared in the center of the room. It kept directly above the lieutenant's head, moving as he moved, vanishing as he looked up.

The note of the violin came into hearing and went out again, repeating this action time and time again.

Sweat dripped off Zen's chin and formed a puddle on the floor under him. He did not know what was happening. Terror that was close to panic was in him but he did not move a muscle. For all he knew, the face might look at him and he might be the next one to vanish.

Where would he find himself if he vanished? *Would* he find himself again? Or did these people slide forever into nothingness, into some dimensional interspace where there was no Earth, no moon, and no stars?

Only he and Nedra were left along the walls.

The others had vanished.

The lieutenant had gone completely crazy. Sputtering a mixture of Chinese and English, he was jabbing his rifle against Nedra's stomach and was yelling at her.

"*Tze!* Go away. I will kill you if you do. *N-oten.* Where did they go? I demand an answer. Speak!"

"I do not know," the girl answered.

"Speak! I command it. Cuso will have my throat slit if I let all of you get away!"

"I have already—"

The lieutenant jabbed the muzzle of his rifle against her stomach.

"If you go away, I will kill you."

He meant what he said.

Smiling at him, the girl vanished.

He pulled the trigger of the weapon. The bullets howled madly through the gallery. Zen dropped hastily to the floor. Death was too close for him to be amazed at the sight of an Asian officer shooting at nothing.

The lieutenant stopped shooting when the magazine was empty. As he clicked another clip into place, some measure of sanity seemed to return to him. He did not shoot the colonel.

Instead Zen found himself being prodded with the muzzle of the still hot and smoking rifle.

"If you go away—"

Zen got to his feet.

"If I knew how to do it, I'd be gone," he said.

"Where did they go? How did they do it?" Fine flecks of spittle were blown from the lieutenant's lips.

The sound of hot lead was still strong in Zen's ears. At any moment, the lieutenant might start shooting again, for any reason. Or for no reason.

"I don't know," Zen said.

"But you've got to know. You're one of them."

"Would I stand around here and let you shoot me if I was one of them?" Zen answered.

Some of the logic of the question must have penetrated to the officer's mad mind. "No. No, you wouldn't. That is, I guess you wouldn't. But you might be trying to trick me." The thought of being tricked seemed to bring all his fury to the surface. "You did it once before, you and the girl."

"How?" Zen demanded.

"You put us all to sleep, you and that girl? Don't tell me you didn't. I was there."

"I was there but I didn't have a damned thing to do with it. And neither did the girl."

"Then who did?"

"West. He was outside with some kind of a sleep generator that operated electronically."

Doubt came over the lieutenant's face. How was he to know if this tall, thin yankee was telling the truth. In his book, all Americans were liars. Why trust this one?

"If you lie to me—"

"I know. You'll shoot me. And I'll return from the other world and strangle you some night, while you sleep."

The shot went home. Like most Asians, this officer was superstitious. Watching the reaction, Zen wondered if this man would ever again dare to go to sleep at night. The deadly *dugphas*, the devil souls of the departed, might strangle him in a spirit noose the instant he closed his eyes.

On the other hand, there was Cuso. The lieutenant *knew* what the Asian leader would do to him. Zen could see him making up his mind that it was better to take a chance on the deadly devils that roam the darkness than on Cuso. The night devils might miss.

"You lie!" The lieutenant lifted the rifle.

At the same instant, Cuso and West entered. The lieutenant lowered the rifle. Hastily he approached his chief and saluted. Then, taking as few chances as possible, he prostrated himself on the floor. Reaching for Cuso's foot, he tried to place it on his neck as a token of submission.

Cuso kicked him in the face. The Asian leader's eyes ranged the room. He saw instantly that his prisoners were missing. His eyes turned green. He kicked the lieutenant in the face again and demanded to know what had happened.

The luckless officer broke into a stream of tight, sing-song language. Now and then he waved his hand as if to say that they had been here but had gone away. "The *dugphas* took them," he screamed in English.

Cuso kicked him in the throat this time. He had no belief in night devils, he did not think they could spirit live people away, and he was not afraid of them.

Another burst of broken, impassioned speech came from the lieutenant's lips. Listening to the sound, watching the contortions in the officer's body, Zen thought with some satisfaction that Ed and Jake were being avenged. Not that they deserved vengeance; they had gotten exactly what was coming to them.

West remained aloof. He glanced around the room but no flicker of surprise showed on his face. Did he know what had happened here? Cuso, listening to his lieutenant, glanced once at the craggy man, a look that was pure suspicious hatred. If it had been possible, Cuso would have had West skinned alive then and there.

Too much was at stake for that. A flayed man could not reveal his secrets. He could only die.

Cuso left off kicking his lieutenant and trying to listen to him at the same time. He turned to West.

"It seems that your people have—departed," he said.

"At least, they do not seem to be here," the craggy man answered. Again his voice had the deep boom of a bell in it.

"That is interesting," Cuso said.

"I find it so," West answered.

"How was it done?"

West spread his hands in a gesture that said something, or nothing. "Perhaps it would be best to ask them."

"You know." The words were a statement, not a question.

"It could be," West answered.

"Then how?" Cuso's words sounded like the snap of a bear trap closing. "I want to know how it was done. No alibis. No evasions. No excuses. Just the truth." The tone of his voice carried the threat of violence with it.

West smiled. "Have I alibied or evaded? Did you not see everything in our center here?"

"I saw many things. That I saw all I do not know."

"You saw what the colonel here—" the craggy man nodded toward Zen, "—called my super radar."

"Did you show him that?" Zen demanded.

"Of course. I have no secrets from the great Asian. Besides, has he not promised me a commission as a marshal in the armed forces of his land?"

The words were easily spoken but Zen knew that West was actually stalling for time. What was he waiting for? Was it the appearance again of the face that had looked from the air in the center of the room? Were the vanished people to reappear, armed with new weapons, and take the Asians prisoners?

"To hell with his commission!" Zen shouted. "He'll never make good on his promise."

"Shut up, both of you!" Cuso shouted. His voice was a bull bellow of sound that roared back from the walls of the gallery and was echoed from the tunnels that led outward. "You are stalling. You are trying to trick me."

West was silent.

"My dog here says the people vanished." Cuso kicked his lieutenant again to indicate who was meant. "Howl, dog!"

The lieutenant obeyed. He was in such a state of mind that if Cuso had told him to die, he would probably have obeyed, as a result of terror and suggestion.

"Do you want to howl like a dog too?" Cuso said to West.

"Really, the possibility does not concern me," the craggy man answered. "Did you have that in mind for me?" The tone was conversational.

"West, this is no time to go over," Zen growled.

"I have no such intention, colonel."

"You admitted once that what you wanted most to do was to join the bronze youth. I'm asking you—"

"*Shut up!*" Cuso screamed. "The next person to open his mouth without my permission I will have shot out of hand."

"Ah," West said.

The Asian leader started to shout an order at his soldiers to shoot the craggy man, then changed his mind as he realized that even though he had the weapons and the men, there was nothing he could gain by killing the goose that might possibly lay a golden egg. As much as he wanted to have West killed, for defying him, he knew he would have to save this pleasure until later.

Cuso swallowed his anger. Since his rage was so great, he had to swallow several times before he got it all down, after which he looked as if he were going to choke on it.

"Look, let's be reasonable," he urged.

"I'm willing," Zen said.

"You're not worth a damn to me!" Cuso shouted.

"He is worth something to me," West interposed.

Again the Asian swallowed. If ever he reached the explosion point, his anger was going to come out as boiling rage. "As I said, let us be reasonable and talk this over together."

"Glad to," West agreed. "What is more reasonable than a corpse?"

The question took Cuso aback. But only for an instant. "Come to think of it, you're right. Nothing that I have ever seen is more agreeable than a corpse, to me, that is. Are you still determined to volunteer for that position, or should I say *condition*?"

"Any time," West answered. "As I told Kurt some time ago, I am rather tired of this plane of existence and I would like to see what it's like over yonder. Not that I don't already know," he added.

"You know what it's like beyond death?" Cuso asked, curious in spite of himself.

"Certainly," West said, in a sure tone of voice.

Listening, Zen again had the impression that the craggy man was stalling for time again. On the other hand, he might be telling the literal truth, he might know what waited at the end of life. If so—Zen let this possibility slide hastily out of his mind. He had more to think about now than he had brain cells to use for the task.

"Then what is it like?" Cuso asked.

"You have heard of heaven—"

"Yes."

"That's where I'm going."

As he spoke, West vanished.

A stunned silence held the big gallery. Cuso, his mouth hanging open, stood leaning forward. On the floor, the lieutenant dared to sit up. He even dared to speak.

"See! That's the way they went. I couldn't stop 'em."

Cuso shouted an order at his men.

Zen found himself tied hand and foot. A raging maniac paced the floor beside him. Every now and then Cuso kicked him. Screaming at the top of his voice, the Asian leader invited Zen to vanish too. It did Zen no good to try to protest that he was not one of the new people and that he knew nothing of the method they had used in disappearing.

In Cuso's mind, he was one of them.

He was to be treated as such.

CHAPTER XIII

At first, the lighted matches under his toe nails hurt like the very devil. He had never known such pain. Then he forgot about the matches under his toe nails. They started lighting them under his fingers.

"Where did they go?" Cuso screamed. "How did they do it?"

Zen had long since ceased trying to say that he didn't know. Instead of speaking, he shook his head. This was all he could do. Cuso interpreted the head shake as a stubborn refusal to answer. He kicked the colonel in the face.

At the kick, the race mind clicked in. This was the effect Zen had—as if a third person had suddenly come in on a party line. After that, the pain from the kick did not seem so important. The torture from the matches under his nails seemed to diminish also.

Not that the contact with the race mind nullified the pain or made it any less real. Fire was still fire and torture was still the same. But neither were very important.

Other things were.

Zen tried to concentrate his attention on the other things. The room, the shouting Cuso, the two Asians who were holding him down while the third thrust the matches under his nails, the shivering Cal, the lieutenant who was over-eager to obey his leader's orders, all these seemed to become misty and vague. These things were real; there was no question about that. But his mind was contacting another reality which made these things different. Time began to lose its meaning.

He wondered if he was fainting. Another question came across his thoughts, heeled over like a sailing ship moving across the wind. Was he dying?

There was no shock with the thought. If that was the way it was, then he was more than ready.

"You are not fainting and you are not dying," the race mind whispered to him. "Come closer to me."

"How do I come closer to you?"

"Let go." The voice of the race mind was like a whisper from the other side of infinity. "Let go and come to me."

Dimly, he wondered how one let go. The answer came with the question. The words meant exactly what they said, the meaning was literal— *let go*.

As he performed the action that went with the words, the big gallery, Cuso, the lieutenant, and the torturers faded away and became a part of a misty world that seemed to have no real existence. Even the pain vanished.

"Come to me," the race mind whispered, again and again, a luring voice that drew him irresistibly.

Abruptly, he was back in the gallery. He did not know how long he had been gone but he realized that some time must have passed, enough to allow them to set up a portable radio transmitter in the gallery. The set looked to be very powerful. A yellow-skinned operator was huddling over the controls.

"In contact with Asian headquarters," Zen thought. He knew his thinking was correct.

Off somewhere in the distance outside the mountain the night shuddered. He knew the meaning of the sound. A rocket ship was either landing or blasting off, probably the latter. A long line of burdened Asians was moving through the gallery.

At the sight of their loads Zen knew what had gone into the hold of that ship. The equipment of the hidden center here. He saw parts of the super radar go past on the backs of sweating Asian soldiers, and he knew where this was going.

At this knowledge, anguish came up in him. With West's super radar in their possession, no American secret was safe from prying Asian eyes, unless some way could be found to shield the frequencies employed.

Such shielding might work for laboratories, but there was no way to shield troop movements and take-offs and landings. These would be as public as an advertisement.

His face was wet. He could not understand this until another bucket of water hit him. An Asian bent over him, saw that his eyes were open, and grunted with satisfaction. They started again on his fingers.

The radio operator called to Cuso, giving him a message. Zen could not understand the language but the Asian leader was both startled and elated. He shouted at the men carrying loads to work faster.

"Not much time left. Big bomb coming."

"What bomb?" Zen thought. With the question came the answer. Warned by Cuso that their preparations were probably known, the Asians had decided to launch their super bomb immediately. Turmoil came up inside Zen at this knowledge.

Real pain came from his finger tips as the torturers began operations again.

"Do you want to die?" the race mind whispered in his thoughts.

Although he couldn't contact it, the race field could reach him. "You have suffered all that is required. You have met the law. You may join me, if you wish."

"I—" Zen shut off his thinking. This was fantasy, the product of torture and nearing dissolution. His own imagination was tricking him, he thought.

"This is not your imagination," the answer came. "This is what you call the race mind."

"But—"

"How do you know? You don't. At this point, you have to accept me on faith." The thinking flowing smoothly into his mind went into silence, then came again, stronger than before. "Do you want to die? You have earned the right."

"No," Zen answered. He screamed the words again. "No. No!"

"The path before you will be difficult."

"I don't care how difficult it is. There's work to be done!" Again he shouted the words.

"Very well. It is your choice. You may remain among the living for as long as your strength may last." The voice whispering in his mind went into silence.

Kurt continued screaming. Pain raced through his consciousness again. As he came awake he realized that he was screaming at the torturer to stop.

He also realized that the Asian had stopped. There was a sound in the gallery. Filling the air, it seemed to emerge from the very walls of the mountain itself.

The note of a violin!

High and sweet and compelling, the sound came from nowhere. Every atom in the solid stone walls seemed to pick it up and to rebroadcast it. The molecules of the air seemed to dance in resonance with it.

Simultaneously, about ten feet above the floor, the face appeared again.

The lieutenant's rifle blasted at it. He fired shot after shot at point blank range. Red-hot slugs howled from the walls of the big gallery in a cacophony of death.

The face smiled at the lieutenant. The lips moved. "Keep shooting, old fellow," the lips seemed to say.

The officer emptied his gun. In a desperate burst of fear, he threw it at the mocking face.

The weapon passed through the face without harming it.

"You fool! That's a projection, not a real person!" Cuso shouted. He grabbed the officer by the shoulder and spun him backward to the floor. "Who are you?" he demanded of the face.

It smiled at him.

Zen repressed the impulse to shout. He knew what was going to happen next.

"I said, *Who are you?*" Cuso shouted again.

The crash of something in the gallery jerked his attention away. Twisting his head around, he saw that one of the soldiers engaged in carrying the loot of this cavern out to the plane waiting to hurry it to Asia, had collapsed on the floor.

Under ordinary circumstances, Cuso would have had the man summarily executed. But with that face smiling at him out of nothing, these circumstances were not ordinary.

Zen, knowing what was going to happen, forgot the pain of his burned fingers and toes. He could feel it creeping over him in waves. This time he did not resist it: He let his eyes close.

When he opened them, the torturer was snoring beside him. Every Asian in the big gallery was sound asleep.

People were crowding around him. The new people. In a sweeping glance, he recognized every person he had met here, except Nedra, and he did not see her at first because she was busy bandaging his hands. West was smiling down at him with an expression that was somehow grandfatherly. But back of West's smile was perturbation.

Zen started to get to his feet and discovered they had not as yet removed the ropes from his legs. As one did this, Nedra clucked reprovingly at him and tried to tell him that he was wounded. He said this did not matter. Faces were here that he did not recognize. This did not matter either.

"You did this?" he said to West.

"Yes. I designed and built the equipment. Others were operating it in this instance." West had something else on his mind.

"Thanks," Zen said. "Why didn't you take me with you when you went—wherever it was you went?"

"We couldn't," West answered. "You haven't had the training."

"Why did you come back?"

"To rescue you. Kurt—" West had something that he wanted to say.

"Nedra, will you stop fussing with me? I'm all right."

"But your poor hands and feet."

"I don't even feel them. I won't have them to feel at all unless action is taken. Don't you understand. Somewhere in Asia they're getting ready to launch a super bomb. Or maybe it's already on its way."

"I didn't know," the girl said. "The big one?"

"Yes."

A flicker of pain crossed her face and she shook her head. "I always wondered what it would be like to live on a mud flat. I wonder if we will be oysters, or eels. Or maybe crabs."

"What the hell are you talking about?" Zen demanded.

"After the bomb goes off," the girl said.

"What then?"

"The race mind will have to start over again," she explained. Her manner indicated that she was explaining something that she clearly understood. She seemed to wonder why he did not understand it. "Maybe we will be turtles? That will be funny! A turtle that can remember when it was a man! That's the way it will be. Except—"

"I know all about that."

"Except that the turtle won't be able to do anything about its memories," the girl continued as if she had not heard him. "It will have flippers and a beak but what it will need will be hands. It won't have them until it grows them itself. A turtle with the memories that it was once a man, knowing that if it had hands, it could rebuild human culture!" A bemused expression appeared on her face. "I wonder how the race mind will solve that problem." Again she seemed to muse. "It would be worse to be crabs. Or would it?"

"Shut up!" Zen snarled. "We're not turtles yet. Or crabs. And we're not back on the mud flats."

"But we're on the edge of them," the girl insisted. "One more teeter and we will go totter."

Zen turned to West. "What the hell has happened to Nedra?"

"Nothing," the craggy man answered. "She has some degree of clairvoyance and it is coming to consciousness. Unfortunately, she has not yet had time to develop her talents in that direction."

"Maybe the turtle wouldn't want to rebuild human culture," the girl interrupted. "Maybe it wouldn't want to go back down that blind alley again. Perhaps it would decide to go into another channel, to develop into something totally different. In that case, it might not need hands."

Zen deliberately ignored her. He turned to West. "A bomb will be going off," he said.

"That is what I've been trying to talk to you about," the craggy man answered. "This is another reason why we came back for you—so we could talk to you about that bomb."

"To me?" Zen said startled.

"Yes, to you."

"Why?"

"Because you are a colonel of intelligence and have experience in such matters. Also because you are something that none of us are—a fighting man."

"I—I don't understand you," Zen answered.

"I can get you there. But once there, my knowledge fails. I, to my regret, know nothing of fighting." West spread his hands in a helpless gesture.

"Get me where?" Zen asked.

"To Asia. To the underground cavern where they are getting ready to launch that bomb," West explained. The tone of his voice said this was easy. The hard part came in knowing what to do, and being able to do it, after they were there.

"To Asia?" Zen parroted the words. He had the dazed impression that this whole scene was unreal, that the snoring Asians on the floor, Cal huddled by the wall, and the new people crowding into the room, would shortly all vanish in puffs of green smoke. "How in the hell will you get us to Asia?"

"How did we get out of this gallery?" West responded. "How did we vanish? How did the men in the reports you read get into the planes that were about to crash? Who landed Colonel Grant's space satellite? Who steered it? Who provided the power to energize the motion? Who—"

"Did you know I knew about Grant?"

"It was obvious that you must know."

"And you can get me to Asia?"

"You and as many others as you choose to take with you!"

Walking over to the sleeping lieutenant, he picked up the man's rifle, then turned to the group.

"Who will go with me to Asia?" he asked.

The group stepped forward as one man.

A knot formed in Kurt Zen's throat at the sight and he gulped to force it down. He knew how much this decision meant to them. They had been trained in the ways of peace, they were searching for the road to the future. Fighting meant turning backward on the path that led to growth, it was the last thing they wanted to do. Yet do it they would, if it was necessary. In an instant they were scrambling for weapons from the sleeping Asians, then they were trying to salute and tell him their names and say they would follow him at the same time.

One man saluted well. "Red-Dog Jimmie Thurman," he said. Pride was in the man's voice.

Zen caught the man's arm. "Red-Dog Jimmie Thurman? But I know you."

"Maybe you do, suh." Thurman spoke with the soft drawl of the old south.

"One of the new people appeared in your plane and saved your life!" Zen burst out.

"Yes, suh. That's right, suh."

"But you deserted!"

"Put it another way, suh, let's say I joined the right side."

"How did you find this place?"

"I just kept thinking and kept trying. Eventually we found each other. The psychos tried to make me believe I was nuts. But I knew better. I knew what had happened. And I knew there had to be a reason for it. I kept hunting until I found that reason. The big part of the battle, where I had an advantage over most everybody else, was that I knew from experience that something was going on. Knowing this much, all I had to do was keep looking." The man's voice drawled the explanation. His eyes smiled. "At your service, suh."

"Do you know that going with me may mean death?"

"What's death, suh?" Red-Dog Jimmie Thurman grinned. "I died over the North Pole, suh."

"Spike Larson," another man said.

"You were in a sub," Zen challenged. A glow was coming up inside of him like nothing he had ever experienced before. He was getting fighting men to stand beside him.

"Yes," Larson answered. "And I will consider it a privilege to stand beside you."

Like soldiers, they passed in review before him, the fat boy, the tall, lean, brown-skinned youths. Somehow he thought there ought to be another one. He looked around for him. Grant was talking to West.

Grant was the man whose face had looked out of thin air in the middle of the room.

Seeing that Zen was staring at him, he left off his talk with the craggy man and came over and saluted.

"How was it up in that satellite?" Zen asked.

"Lonely, as hell, colonel," Grant answered.

"Do you want to go with me to Asia?"

"There's no place on Earth I'd rather go. And, the way things stand now I don't have much choice. If they get that bomb into the air—" He left the sentence unfinished.

Then Nedra was standing in front of Zen. At the sight of her, it seemed to him that the world stood still. He shook his head.

"Why?" she challenged.

"Because I love you," he answered.

"Then that is the real reason why you should take me with you," she answered.

"I don't follow," he said.

"If you fail, there will be no tomorrow," she answered. To her, the statement had no answer. "Besides, I am a nurse," she continued. "If there are wounded, I can help with them."

"But—"

"The fact that you love me does not enter into this situation. It is a thing apart. It is a very wonderful thing," she added hastily, the star light shining in her eyes. "And I wish we could bring it to fruit the ways it used to be. But those days are gone. And I am going to Asia with you."

Watching, West smiled. Zen spread his hands in a gesture of defeat. He turned to the craggy man. "This sleep thing: I don't know how you do it and don't much care, but you obviously have a portable generator of some kind that you used to put the lieutenant out in the ghost town."

"Yes," West agreed.

"I'd like to borrow the unit," Zen said.

"Gladly, colonel. I wish we had other weapons."

"We'll make do with what we have," Zen answered.

CHAPTER XIV

"Zero minus one hour," the loudspeaker droned, in a Chinese dialect.

In a deep cavern in the hinterlands of Asia, men responded to the command coming over the speaker system. Already driven to the point of exhaustion, they were working harder than they had ever worked before. The moment of victory, for which all true Asians had lived, was near at hand. The launching of this bomb would make the Asian Union master of the world. Orders had come through to launch this bomb immediately.

"Zero minus forty-five minutes," the speaker said. The drone had gone from the voice of the officer watching the time. A rising excitement appeared in the tones as if he, too, had caught the scent of fear rising in the vast underground depot.

So much was left to be done. The atomic warhead was already in place, waiting for the day of launching, otherwise the task would have been impossible. The driving engines were complete, but had to be fueled. The steering equipment was almost ready, only the installation of the left gyroscope was necessary. This was at hand waiting to be installed. Five technicians constantly got in each other's way as they tried to slip the delicate instrument into place.

"Zero minus thirty minutes!"

The gyroscope was eased into place and tested. It was found to be in perfect working order.

In the course plotting room, the final calculations were being made. Wind direction and velocity aloft had been noted across half the planet. This had some importance on the launching and landing end but had no significance when the bomb itself was out of the atmosphere.

The target had been figured and refigured. Actually, the target was anywhere on the continent of North America. If this bomb struck anywhere in the Mississippi valley, the whole watershed below the striking point would be scoured clean of all life. Water carrying radiation downstream would account for that.

"Zero minus fifteen minutes!"

On the outside of the mountain, in a special observatory constructed for this precise purpose, radar scopes for tracking the rocket were ready. Instruments in the laboratory there were for the purpose of changing the course of the super bomb, if it veered too far from its destination. The technicians there were on their toes. They had no guards to encourage them but they needed none. They knew what would happen if this bomb failed to land and the fault was traced to their door.

What would happen when the bomb landed?

Hell would happen!

Probably the crust of the Earth would open up in a hole miles in depth. Meteor Crater, in Arizona, would be the work of a child compared to the result of this explosion. What had happened at Hiroshima and Nagasaki would be nothing in comparison.

The possibility existed that the molten magma of the core of the planet would gush forth. No one knew for sure whether or not this would happen. If it did take place, the result might be the sudden appearance of a lake of over-flowing lava.

The shock waves from the bomb would probably be strong enough to pull down every skyscraper that still remained standing in America.

The effect on the watershed where the bomb landed would be almost complete catastrophe. If it struck on any of the rivers or streams flowing into the Mississippi, the water supply of all cities downstream to New Orleans would be contaminated.

Nobody knew what the effect of the fall-out from this bomb would be. High air currents might carry radioactive particles for thousands of miles from the explosion point, where they would fall as a gentle but very deadly rain upon the Earth below.

"Zero minus ten minutes!"

The high, thin note of a violin appeared in the vast underground cavern. Amid the scurrying of feet, the shouts of the foremen bossing the work gangs, and the occasional cracking of the rifles of the guard, the sound was unheard by the ears. But deeper centers heard it.

The first man to go was a fat engineer. Sighing, he stumbled and fell. When he did not rise a guard approached him. As the guard determined that the man was snoring, he lifted his rifle.

The engineer died without awakening.

Another shot rang out as another man went to sleep, then continued on to join his fathers.

The technician busy filling the fuel tanks of the rocket was the third man to go. He managed to finish closing the filler cap and to lay down his flexible line before the urge to sleep overcame him.

By this time the guards knew that something was wrong.

Silence came over the cavern. In the stillness, the note of the violin flickering up and down the scale could be heard. Men looked at each other in growing apprehension. Looking, some of them lay down and went to sleep.

"Sleep gas!" an officer bawled. "Shoot all foreigners on sight!"

The officer suspected that some spy had slipped into the underground cavern and had released gas there. His command was intended to enable his men to find and eliminate this alien. As such, from a military standpoint, it was a good command. It had this deficiency: when his men did not find any aliens, but their own people continued going to sleep on them, they began imagining foreigners. The guards began to shoot their own technicians and engineers.

As panic swept through the cavern, guards began to shoot other guards. Soon the people in this huge underground chamber were tearing and destroying each other. And one other thing: they were also going to sleep.

The panic grew to hurricane proportions.

When Kurt Zen appeared inside the cavern the whole vast place was as still as a tomb. Smoke from the rifles hung in the air, the cavern stank of death and fear. But the bomb still rested in its launching cradle.

Zen took one long look at that bomb. He felt his sigh of relief clear down to the ends of his toes. At the sight, the last remnant of pain vanished from his toes and fingers. Not that the damage done by the matches did not still exist. It did. But in the surge of elation that swept through him, he completely forgot the pain.

"We just got here in time," a man said, appearing beside him. It was Spike Larson who had spoken. Awe on his face, Larson glanced around the cavern. "They started killing each other. They must have gone nuts."

"I don't blame them," Zen said. "I damned near did, on the way here."

"That trip through nothing is sure a stinker, isn't it," Larson answered, grinning and shaking his head.

Zen agreed with him whole-heartedly. After tuning his body to an instrument in the cavern, hidden so well that Cuso's men had not had time to find it, West had punched a button. The machine had vanished. West had vanished. A horrible moment had come when it had seemed that his feet were standing on nothing more substantial than air. What he had felt under his feet had, in fact, been far less substantial than air, which had body. It had been even less solid than space. It had been *nothing*.

Swishing, colonel Grant came into existence on the other side of Zen. Grant looked fussed, but he gripped the rifle he had taken from one of Cuso's men with determination.

"Just between you and me, I'd rather fly a space satellite to Mars any day in preference to facing this jump."

"I know what you mean," Zen said.

As he spoke, another figure came into existence to his left. Nedra! She came spinning into reality with a smile on her face. Zen wasted a moment wondering what kind of cast-iron nerves this girl had.

"It looks as if all we have to do is to tie them up," Spike Larson said. "This is almost too good to be true."

"It is too good to be true," Zen said. Turmoil was—somewhere. He did not know where but it seemed to him that a vast uneasiness had suddenly come into existence. It had to do, somehow, with the future, with a something that was about to happen.

"Halt!" Grant's voice rang out.

Zen swung his gaze around just in time to see an Asian lift himself to his feet near a control board that stood beside the rocket.

"He's walking in his sleep," Larson exclaimed.

"*Zero minus one minute*," the loudspeaker announced.

"Where in the hell is that man on the speaker?" Grant demanded. "The sleep frequency didn't get to him!"

"No time to be concerned about him now," Zen said. The turmoil that existed somewhere had increased in intensity. Somehow it was concerned with the solitary Asian who was reeling in circles like a drunken man trying to make up his mind.

"Shall I shoot him, colonel?" Grant demanded.

Zen hesitated. He knew that West's deepest wish was to avoid violence if that was possible.

The split second's delay was fatal. Grant's shot rang out—much too late.

Reeling on his feet, the man reached the control panel, and pulled the single switch there. A heavy thud came from the rocket as a ram drove home inside the heavy metal hull.

"Get back!" Zen screamed.

He caught Nedra and pulled her backward. Beside him, he knew that Grant and Larson were also reeling backward. Inside the rocket a steady rumble of sound was building up. Low in frequency but heavy in volume it seemed to shake the foundations of the Earth itself. Inside the vessel heavy heat charges were building up. Smoke and flame spurted backward as the first warming charge let go.

For all Zen knew this section was to have been cleared before the firing of the first rocket. He did not know whether provision had been made for the elimination of flame and smoke but he knew that heat and smoke hit him as he pulled Nedra away.

Then the main charges let go.

Rising like some devil spurting upward from the depths of hell it-self, the launching cradle carrying the rocket lurched upward. The stone floor shook underfoot, the mountain shook. Unless this rocket could be stopped, the whole planet would shake. Earth would twitch her skin like an elephant stung by a giant wasp.

With a thundering roar the rocket shook itself loose from its cradle and hurled into the sky under its own power.

"West," Zen shouted.

"Yes, Kurt." The craggy man's reply was as prompt as it would have been if he had stayed in the same room. Actually he was in the American center.

"We've lost," Zen said.

"I know," West replied. A sadness as deep as the ocean of space was in his voice.

"Pull these people back to you."

"Of course."

"Me last." The last lingering roars of sound were still pounding down the bore of the launching cradle.

"Why do you want to be last?"

"Duty," Zen said. "Get that miracle device of yours into operation, pronto."

"Sure. I'm starting now."

"Hey, guys, you're going home!" Zen yelled at the people with him.

"What good is it to go home?" Spike Larson asked.

"There won't be any home within an hour," Grant added. "Or how-ever long that rocket will take to land. Why go back to what isn't there?"

"That's where we will start the task of rebuilding," Zen said.

"Rebuild what with what?" Larson demanded.

"There will be something left," Zen said firmly. "You are already un-derground. You will stay that way. Keep the good fight going, for years. Raise some kids to keep it going after you are gone." He felt very firm and sure about what he was saying.

"You're full of hot air," Red-Dog Jimmie Thurman said.

"Besides, you are planning something else," Nedra spoke. "You want to get rid of us so you can—"

"West!" Zen shouted.

"Yes, Kurt."

"Take 'em away!" Zen yelled. "They're trying to rebel on me. Take Nedra first before she reads my mind."

"I'm working as fast as I can," West answered. "This instrument has to be tuned to the individual body frequency. Ah—"

"I knew there was something—" Nedra began. And vanished. Zen grinned. He had the impression that she was calling him names that no lady should speak as she went away. Time would cure that, if any time was left. In the chamber an Asian was stirring.

"Zen, old man, what are you up to?" Grant asked.

"Take this one next," Kurt ordered. Grant looked reluctant but resigned as he disappeared.

Zen was alone in the big chamber. Smoke swirled from the ceiling. One Asian was already on his feet and a guard was sitting up.

"I've got them all here," West's voice came across vast distances.

"Good."

"Are you ready?"

"Yeah," Zen answered. "But I'm going that way." He pointed toward the ceiling.

"Kurt!" West's voice was sharp with sudden pain as he caught the colonel's meaning.

"That way or no way," Zen answered.

"But that's not a passenger rocket."

"The hull will hold enough air to keep me alive for as long as I need to be there."

"But the rocket is in constantly accelerating flight. It's a moving target."

"Red-Dog Jimmie Thurman's plane was falling and Colonel Grant's satellite was moving and Spike Larson's sub was on the bottom of the Indian Ocean. Don't give me any back talk, Sam. Somebody got into that plane and that satellite and that submarine. I can get into that rocket. You're the man who can put me there."

"But I'm not on that target!" West's voice had a wail in it.

"Then get on it!" Kurt Zen sounded like an exceedingly gruff drill sergeant addressing a new recruit, or like a colonel who had his mind made up.

"All right. I'll do my best. But something will remain here, Kurt, even after the explosion. We'll be safe, in a way, here."

"That argument has already been used, by me, to get the others back to you. You and I know, Sam, that hell won't hold a hat to the American continent if that whizzer hits."

"All right," West repeated. "Ah! I'm on the rocket as a target."

"Good!" Zen repressed every muscular tremor everywhere in his body.

Somewhere there was jubilation, a sensed but not tangible vibration that he could not locate. He concentrated on the jubilation.

A layer of smoke floated down from the ceiling like a descending death-pall. The guard had gotten to his feet. He had picked up his rifle and was staring around the room seeking either an explanation for what had happened, or a target. To him, which he got didn't matter. His eyes came to focus on the lean colonel with the bandaged fingers. That uniform did not belong here.

The guard raised his rifle.

"Good luck, Kurt," West's voice whispered across the space between two continents.

As the gun exploded in his face, Kurt Zen felt his body vibrate into what seemed to be nothing. Again the terror wrenched at his soul. Again he experienced the mind-compelling agony of this incredible type of space flight.

This time he did not mind these terrors. Somewhere in his mind was jubilation. Wondering if it was the forerunner of death, he continued to concentrate on that.

Dimly, as if from some other space, or some other time, he was aware of a roar. The rocket swam into existence ten feet away from him. He was outside it, in airless space.

West had made a miscalculation.

Agony seared every cell in his body. Pain clamped at his throat like hands trying to choke him to death.

"Oops! I made a mistake," he heard West gasp.

He was moving with the rocket, on a parallel course. West had matched course and velocity but he had not achieved his exact aiming point. Error in the instrument? Human mistake? Who knew?

Who cared?

Click!

Like a vast ocean of warm, pulsing, sure power, the race mind came into Kurt Zen. It existed here in space, too! He had never thought of that. In what little thinking he had had time to do, he had considered it as a super special sort of field which possessed intelligence but which was limited to the surface of the planet.

Here in space, it sustained life in him.

He did not know how this was done, this was one of the mysteries which must be left to the future to solve—if there was a future other than the mud flats. It felt to him as if a vast tidal current was flowing into his body.

Click!

He was in the rocket!

The smell of overheated oil fouled his nose. As he tried to move, he bumped his head. He was in a narrow passage. Ahead was a control panel with automatic devices. He began to crawl in that direction.

Noise was a thundering roar in his ears. His whole body felt as if it was about to shake to pieces. The passage was narrow. It had never been intended for humans. Moving upward, Zen found it was too narrow. He got stuck.

No matter how hard he tried he could not move an inch forward. The control panel was so close he could spit on it but it could not have been farther out of his reach if it had been on the other side of the Moon.

Air was getting short. He twisted and squirmed, fighting like the devil, but his body was wedged into the narrow passage in such a way that he could not move.

Something pulled at his arms. Nedra was directly ahead of him. She was trying to pull him forward along the passage.

"You?" he whispered.

"Who has a better right than I?" she answered. Sweat grimed her face. Her hair was awry. Fiercely she pulled at him.

The rocket yawed, beginning its turn in space. He forced himself forward. And came free.

Somehow he found the strength to pull himself up in front of the control panel. He was running on nervous energy now and he knew it. No strength was left in his body beyond what he was forcing into it.

"Send it out to space!" he muttered. "Send it out there!" He tried to wave his arm in an outward gesture and bumped his hand on the steel hull.

Light came through a circular port. He had a glimpse of the Earth down below. The planet was very far away. Blue seas and green land, the planet was also very beautiful.

He fumbled his way over the controls, trying to understand them. Somewhere stabilizing gyroscopes were running smoothly. He could hear them. The controls were simple. He decided which way was up, and jammed home the controls.

Nothing happened.

In the confined quarters his laughter had madness in it.

Nedra stared at him.

"What happened?"

"Nothing. Nothing happened. They're locked in place."

His eyes grew very wide.

"These controls are only for establishing the flight course. Once that is established and the rocket launched, they automatically lock in place."

"Then we can't change the course?"

"No."

Her face puckered and she looked like a small girl about to cry.

Another panel to the left caught his attention. It had a red button on it. He studied the wiring on it.

"By thunder!" the words burst involuntarily from his lips.

"What is it, Kurt?"

"They put a manual control on the warhead. It's got to be that. It can't be anything else." He pointed to the red button. "Why do you suppose they did that?"

"Test purposes, probably, to check the firing mechanism before the warhead was installed. What difference does it make?" Nedra's voice was listless.

"Maybe we can go to heaven."

"What do you mean?"

He explained very carefully what he meant.

"Explode the rocket here in space?"

"Sure," he said. His tone of voice said this was nothing, that anybody could do it. West's voice clamored in his mind again. He ignored it. His hand moved toward the red button.

"There's one thing I want you to know," he said, pausing.

"What is that?"

"I love you," he said.

She came into his arms like a tired, frightened child. "I knew that the minute I saw you," she said. He held her close to him and she lay there, seemingly very content. "All right," she said. "I'm ready." Her lips sought his.

Kissing her, he reached behind her back and punched the red button.

A relay thudded.

Darkness closed in.

* * * *

Kurt Zen came out of that darkness to find himself staring upward into the face of Sam West. There was something about that face that was familiar, something that he should have guessed long before. He tried to think what it was.

"How'd you get to heaven?" he said.

"The warhead had a delay relay on it," West explained. "It was about thirty seconds, as near as I can figure it. Anyhow it gave us just enough time to snatch both of you out of that rocket before she blew."

What he said sounded very important. Under other circumstances, Zen knew he would have considered it important. But other things seemed more significant now. "Did she blow?" he asked.

"All of ten minutes ago," West said exultantly. "Do you know what this means, Kurt? Do you know what it means?"

"Yeah," Zen answered. "I won't have to be an eel." There was still this other thing that was important. "Say—"

"An eel?" For an instant the craggy man was puzzled. Then he grasped the meaning. "You're right, Kurt. No eels—for any of us."

"That's good," Zen said. "Nedra—"

"She's right here beside you, still out from exhaustion. But she will be all right."

"Good," Zen said again. This other fact was still in his mind. As he tried to think what it was, the answer came to him. He looked up at the craggy man. "You're not Sam West," he said.

"No?" the craggy man said, the ghost of a smile on his lips. "Then who am I?"

"You're Jal Jonner. Nobody but Jal Jonner could have done all the things you have done."

"You're right, Kurt. I'm Jal Jonner. And you're Kurt Zen. And this is Nedra—" Zen saw the smile on the face of the craggy man. It was a very good smile, the best he had ever seen. Then it faded away as he sank into the deep slumber of exhaustion. He did not even feel Jonner place Nedra's hand in his as he went to sleep.